THE MURDER LIST

An enthralling crime mystery full of twists

ROGER SILVERWOOD

Yorkshire Murder Mysteries Book 24

JOFFE BOOKS

Revised edition 2021
Joffe Books, London
www.joffebooks.com

First published in Great Britain in 2015

ISBN: 978-1-78931-700-8

ONE

DI Michael Angel's office, Bromersley Police Station, South Yorkshire
Tuesday, 5 May 2015, 8.28 a.m.

The phone rang. The detective inspector reached out for it.

'Angel,' he said.

'Control, sir, DS Clifton. I've got a triple nine suspected murder, just come in.'

Angel blinked. He quickly picked out a scrap of paper to write on from the pile of letters, papers, reports and envelopes piled up on the desk in front of him. Then he picked up his pen.

'Fire away, Bernie,' he said.

'Body of a woman aged about sixty,' Clifton said, 'name of Gladys Grant in a corner shop at 83 Sebastopol Terrace, that's off Canal Street. Reported by a Mrs Edith Beasley of 180 Canal Street, a customer. First report received at 8.25 a.m. Patrol car and paramedic notified and despatched. That's it, sir.'

Angel wrinkled his nose. 'Advise SOCO, Dr Mac, DS Carter and DS Crisp. Tell them I want them at the scene ASAP. And ask DI Asquith to provide two PCs for security duties there.'

'Right, sir.'

'I'm on my way,' Angel said and he replaced the phone.

Angel drove the BMW slowly along Sebastopol Terrace, not wanting to drive past the little shop. He soon came up to number 83 and the dilapidated sign, P. Grant. High Class Groceries and Provisions, and stopped the BMW. He noticed the sign in the door window informing him that the shop was open.

He quickly reached forward to the glove compartment and took out a thin, sealed white paper packet. He tore off the top and took out a pair of elasticised rubber gloves. He put them on, got out of the car, locked it and crossed the pavement to the shop door and went in.

There was a short, rotund woman standing there, looking as if she preferred to be somewhere else. They looked at each other.

Angel said, 'Did *you* send for the police, love?'

She looked relieved. 'Yes. At last. Oh, I thought you was never coming. I have been waiting here on my own for ages. Absolute ages.'

'You reported a body?'

'Yus. Gladys Grant. She's on the floor. Behind the counter.' She tossed her head in that direction. 'Dead as a dodo. It's awful. Never seed anything like it.'

Angel peered over the counter. In the small space, he saw the figure of a small woman with mousey-coloured hair, wearing an apron over a floral dress. The body was in a sitting position on the shop floor. Her hands were on her lap and she seemed to be holding something. He couldn't be sure, but he thought it was a cauliflower. Her back was supported against wooden packing cases positioned on their sides which constituted makeshift shelving. The packing cases were crammed full of tinned and boxed foods.

He strained further over the counter to see as much as he could. There were no signs of a weapon or a showing of blood or anything else unusual or irregular.

He turned back to the woman. 'You must be Mrs Beasley,' he said. 'You found the body?'

She blinked, breathed in, stuck out her ample chest and said, 'Yes.'

Angel nodded, pursed his lips and said, 'On your way here, did you see anybody leaving the place?'

'No.'

The shop door opened. It was DS Taylor, head of SOCO at Bromersley. He was dressed in the obligatory disposable white paper suit and blue Wellingtons.

'Good morning, sir,' Taylor said.

There was hardly room in the shop at that side of the counter for the three of them.

'Good morning, Don,' Angel said, then he looked back at the short, corpulent woman and said, 'We'd better go outside, Mrs Beasley. Give them a bit of room.' Then he turned back to DS Taylor and said, 'The victim is on the floor at the other side of the counter. I haven't been round there. Seems to be holding a cauliflower . . . ? Can't think that's right.'

Taylor frowned. 'Sounds funny, sir. A cauliflower? I'll have a good look.'

Angel ushered Mrs Beasley out of the shop and suggested that they could talk in his car.

She felt important as she climbed into the passenger seat and Angel closed the door. He went round the car to the driver's door and was soon seated beside her.

'You know, Inspector,' she began, shaking all her chins, '*I* thought it was a cauliflower she was holding. Why on earth would she want to be holding a cauliflower?'

Angel shook his head. 'No idea. Now then, Mrs Beasley, please tell me all that has happened this morning.'

'Well, I didn't sleep very well, last night, Inspector. But I woke up about eight o'clock, and I was desperate for a fag. You know how it is. So I scratched around and got two quid together. I knew that that would buy me some. I got washed and threw on my clothes. I knew that Gladys Grant usually opened the shop up at about eight. I suppose it's to catch folk on their way to work. I only live a few doors away, and I was *that* relieved when I saw that the open sign was showing. Anyway, I pushed open the shop door. The shop bell rang out enough to waken the dead. But nobody came. I thought maybe Cliff, her son, would serve me. He came home yesterday. He'd been away a year or so.'

Angel's eyebrows went up. 'You knew him?' he said.

She smiled. 'Oh yes. Known him since he was a little lad. Went to school with my lad. But he wasn't much for schooling, wasn't Cliff. Whereas my son Benjamin went to uni and got himself a degree. He's now got a big job in Northampton. Eight hundred people under him.'

'So the dead woman's son is called Cliff Grant?'

'Yes. Oh, I've just thought,' she said. 'He'll cop for the shop and all Gladys Grant's money, won't he?'

Angel shrugged. 'I don't know.'

'Oh, I think he will,' Mrs Beasley said. 'She's no closer relations I've heard of. There hasn't been a Mr Grant for twenty years at least. Might be longer.'

'Well, where is he now, this Cliff Grant?'

'Don't know,' she said. 'No idea.'

'How old is he?'

'He'll be about thirty, same age as my Benjamin.'

'Could he be at work?'

She smiled. 'I'd be very surprised if he's in work, Inspector. Cliff's not very keen on work. Anyway, if he'd got a decent job, I don't think he'd come back here.'

'Why not?'

'Well, Inspector, Gladys Grant was no bundle of joy. She was mean and she'd have worked him like a workhorse. He wouldn't have stuck it. Oh no. Cliff wasn't interested in hard work. He has always taken what had seemed to him to be the easiest way. When you meet him, you'll see what I mean. He's positively lovely. He's a proper lady's man. A very handsome young chap. I mean, if there was any mistletoe about, I wouldn't have minded going under it with him, if I was years younger.'

Angel wasn't in the mood for frivolity. He was far too worried. 'Well, where is he *now*?' he said. 'That's what I'd like to know.'

Mrs Beasley looked at Angel and frowned. 'I think that *you* think that he might have done it, don't you?' she said. 'Like they had had some row about something.'

'No, no, no. I don't know anything yet.'

'Well, she could be very aggravating, I can tell you. But he wouldn't kill her. Cliff wouldn't harm a fly.'

Angel licked his lips with the tip of his tongue. He had come across some of the nicest, mildest men who normally wouldn't harm a fly, but along came somebody — frequently a relative — who pressed the wrong button on the wrong day and released a monster that had been shackled far too long.

'Thank you, Mrs Beasley,' Angel said. 'I may come back to you if anything else crops up.'

'Righto, Inspector. Call on me anytime if there's anything I can do to help.'

Angel went round to the passenger side of the car, assisted Edith Beasley out of the car and watched her waddle along Canal Street.

At that moment, the glamorous member of Angel's team arrived in a small, unmarked Ford car. She saw Angel, parked her car behind his, got out and came up to him. It was Detective Sergeant Carter.

'Good morning, sir,' she said. 'Got your message. Are we on a murder?'

'Ah. Looks like it, Flora,' Angel said. 'The proprietor of this shop was apparently murdered either during the night or early this morning. Start the door to door, lass. See if anybody was around. I'm particularly interested in the son, Cliff.'

'Right, sir,' she said and turned away.

'And Flora,' he called. She looked back. 'Seen anything of Crisp?'

'No, sir,' she said, unable to conceal a smile. 'I don't expect he'll be long.'

Angel wrinkled his nose.

DS Carter went off to begin her inquiries.

Detective Sergeant Crisp was always missing, always late, always prepared with a list of excuses and implausible explanations.

Just then, Angel saw another unmarked car he recognized as a police car coming along Sebastopol Terrace towards the shop. He was pleased to see that the driver was Trevor Crisp. On this occasion he was . . . surprisingly almost prompt.

Angel waited outside the shop door for the sergeant to park the car and make his way to him.

'Good morning, sir,' Crisp said with a smile.

'One of these days you'll actually be on time,' Angel said.

'You can't say I'm late this time, sir. I only knew about the call eight minutes ago.'

Angel shook his head, puckered his lips and blew out a metre of air and let him win the round.

'There's a woman apparently murdered in there,' Angel said. 'Until uniformed arrive, will you guard this door? I expect there'll be customers and nosey parkers flocking round. When uniformed can take over from you, I want you to liaise with Flora and assist her with the door to door. She's already started on Sebastopol Terrace.'

Crisp shrugged. 'All right, sir.'

Angel sensed that the sergeant didn't seem to like the job of door to door. Probably thought it was demeaning.

'That's very important work, Crisp,' Angel said. 'We might pick up the sighting of the murderer or a witness . . . who knows?'

'Yes, sir.'

Angel turned back to the shop door, pressed the handle down and went inside.

At the sound of the door closing, Taylor and a DC also in whites looked up and across the counter. They were still working around the body.

'What you got then, Don?' Angel said.

Taylor said, 'She's certainly dead, sir. There are several wounds in her heart. She's lost a fair bit of blood.'

Angel wrinkled his nose.

'*You* wouldn't have seen it, sir,' Taylor said, 'because of the cauliflower.'

Angel responded by filling his cheeks with air and frowning. 'Appalling,' he said. After a moment or two, he said, 'What do you reckon the cauli's all about, Don?'

'No idea, sir.'

'Is there any sign of how the killer gained access?'

'No signs of a break in, sir. All downstairs windows and doors sound as a bell.'

The shop door rattled. Angel turned towards it. The door opened and a short man also in whites came in. He was carrying a Gladstone bag.

It was Dr Mac. Although he had lived in England most of his life, he spoke with an accent that would instantly have informed all Scotsmen and many others that he was a Glaswegian.

Angel always liked to tease the old Scot. 'Good morning, Mac,' he said. 'Where have you been? Don Taylor and his team have been here hours.'

'So there you are again, Michael Angel, with your untruths,' Mac said. 'I happen to know that they've been here about ten minutes. You don't catch an old soldier out as easily as that.'

Angel grinned. 'How do you know that?'

'I happened to ask your sergeant on the door, young Crisp, on my way in,' Mac said with a teasing twinkle in his eye. 'You're not the only detective in the camp, you know.'

Angel smiled. 'I thought you'd been having an extra wee portion of porridge maybe to celebrate Robbie Burns's birthday.'

Mac looked at him. 'I *did* have an extra portion of porridge this morning, Michael, but it was to fortify me to come out and solve the puzzles you set me. And as a matter of fact, this is the 5 May. Robbie Burns birthday is 25 January as every true Scot will tell you.'

Angel smiled then nodded. The smile left him as the seriousness of the situation prevailed. 'A woman was stabbed and died holding a cauliflower, Mac. That's this morning's puzzle.'

The doctor's eyebrows shot up. 'Really?' he said.

Taylor and the detective constable stood up.

'You can come round here now, Doctor,' Taylor said. 'There isn't much room, but we've done all we can do here until she can be moved.'

'Thank you, Don,' Mac said.

The two SOCO officers then went into the sitting room.

Dr Mac looked at Angel, who gestured with an open hand the narrow door in the counter between the customer side and the serving side of the tiny shop. 'Through here, Mac,' he said.

Mac raised his bag chest high and squeezed through, accidentally catching the corner of a box of Shredded Wheat, which rocked and caused the few boxes above it to sway. Nothing fell.

When he was on the other side, Mac stood there and looked at the body for a few seconds. He had seen hundreds, maybe thousands of dead bodies in his experience but he was always in awe of the first sight of a body that had been murdered.

The shop door behind Angel opened and Crisp looked in. He looked at Angel. 'Oh, there you are, sir. There's the son out here. He insists on coming in. He's asking me all sorts of questions.'

Angel's face muscles tightened then relaxed. 'All right, Trevor, I'll see him.'

Crisp went outside back onto the pavement, followed by Angel. He closed the shop door.

A tall, smart, well-dressed, some would say handsome, Cliff Grant came up to Angel.

Crisp said, 'This is Mr Grant, sir.'

The young man was well-groomed and wore a smart suit, collar and tie. He looked at Angel with soft blue eyes, both angry and afraid.

'Are you in charge?' he said. 'I really want to speak to whoever's in charge.'

'I'm in charge, Mr Grant,' Angel said.

'Well, what is happening? What are all these police cars doing here? Why can't I get into my own home? Why won't anybody tell me anything?'

TWO

Twenty minutes later, Cliff Grant was on the settee in the living room of the shop, holding a brandy glass containing less than a finger's worth of the golden liquid. He was sipping the last of his late mother's private bottle taken from the sideboard cupboard. His bronzed face was lined and weary. He kept rubbing his forehead with his hand.

Sitting opposite him was Angel. In front of him he had an envelope he made notes on that he kept in the inside pocket of his jacket. He sat there, with pen in hand, patiently waiting . . . waiting to ask questions.

'Are you ready now, Mr Grant?' Angel said.

'Yes, Inspector. It's been such a shock.'

'Well, in your own time, tell me everything you did this morning.'

'Yes. Certainly. I'll try,' he said. 'Let me see. I was asleep in my room just above the shop here. First thing I remember, I was being shaken and called. It was Ma, she was telling me to get up. She said that I had a lot to do. I don't know what time it was. I didn't have a watch or a clock. But it was early. Well, I knew I had a lot to do. She was already dressed. She said she was going down to start breakfast, that the bathroom was free and I was to get up and get washed, shaved, dressed and come down. Well, I was halfway through shaving when she called up that my breakfast was out and going cold. I finished shaving and went downstairs. Anyway, when I finished breakfast, she said I was to get dressed and set off to the hairdresser in town as soon as possible. Then I had to walk the two miles or so to town to the Job Centre.'

Angel looked up from his notes and said, 'So what time did you leave the shop?'

'Must have been about eight o'clock.'

'And was your mother all right when you left her?'

Grant looked up. His lips tightened. He didn't like the question. 'Of *course* she was all right. What do you mean?'

'What was she doing? I assume she was busy with something.'

'She was always busy with something. She was clearing the breakfast table, putting the dirty pots in the sink . . . and so on.'

'Was the shop door open for business?'

'Yes. I went out that way. It was nearer than going out the back.'

'What about the back door?'

'That was always locked when the shop was open anyway. It was a rule she had made. She had once been robbed when an accomplice of a young thief took her attention in the shop. She wasn't leaving herself open for it to happen again.'

'Yes,' Angel said slowly as he rubbed his chin. 'And you're sure that nobody else was in the house or shop when you left at eight o'clock, and that your mother was alive?'

Cliff Grant's jaw dropped open. He looked slowly round the living room. 'Look here, Inspector, that's the second time you've hinted that I might have . . .' He broke off, swallowed and continued. 'I know that my mother and I didn't altogether hit it off. She was very difficult, and we didn't seem to get on well, but I wouldn't, I couldn't do anything to hurt her. When I left the house to go to the hairdresser's and the shops, she was fine. She was a bit put out by me, but she was absolutely fine.'

Angel nodded several times. Grant wasn't certain that he believed him.

'Very well,' Angel said. 'And what time did you arrive at the hairdresser's?'

'Must have been about 8.40. It took me all of forty minutes to walk from here to there.'

'Which hairdresser's did you go to?'

'Harry Rosen on Market Street. I was his first customer, I think, this morning. Anyway, I didn't have to wait. As I went in, I sat down in the chair and he started cutting straightaway. Never happened like that before.'

'How long were you in there?'

'Ten or fifteen minutes at most. Then I went to the Job Centre. I was in there about ten minutes, I suppose. But I wasn't timing myself. I looked along the cards at Job Opportunities. Either I wasn't qualified for it, or it was a long way away, in Ethiopia or Elgin, or I needed my own car, or it was part-time, or I had to have a German shepherd dog, bring it home, look after it, feed it and work with it. That was for security work all night at the Glass Works. I couldn't do any of those, so I went to the desk and asked if all the available jobs they had were on show. I was told that they were, so I came out.'

Angel looked up from his notes, nodded and said, 'That would be about ten or fifteen minutes past nine. Then what did you do?'

'I went to the other end of Market Street to Jeeves, the jeweller's, and bought this watch.' He pulled up the sleeve of his jacket and showed Angel a bright, shiny yellow watch with matching bracelet.

Angel looked at it and said, 'Very nice, Mr Grant.'

Grant beamed. 'Yes,' he said. 'It cost me four hundred and twenty pounds.'

'Where did you get all that money from?' Angel said.

Grant blinked. 'Ma gave it me. She told me to go and get a watch, and get a good one, she said.'

'And how long were you in the jeweller's?'

'Oh, about ten minutes, I should think.'

'That would take you up to about twenty to twenty-five minutes past nine.'

'Then I came back here,' Grant said. His mood changed. He looked at the rocking chair. 'To this.' Then he looked down. 'Ma gone. Now it's me on my own.' He stood up, pushed his hands in his trouser pockets and meandered around the rocking chair.

Angel thought he saw Grant's eyes moisten.

Angel said, 'Making your way back here . . . must have taken twenty or twenty-five minutes. That means you would have been back around nine forty or nine fifty. The time now is ten past ten. That's right, you've been here with me about twenty minutes, haven't you?'

'I don't know how I'm going to manage, Inspector,' Grant said as he pulled and twisted a tuft of his hair. 'I mean, I don't know anything about running a shop.'

Angel frowned, pursed his lips and said, 'The principle of business is the same. You make or buy something that people want for, say, two pounds. You sell it for three, making sure that your expenses aren't more than a pound.'

But Grant wasn't happy. 'That's not *all* there is to it, Inspector,' he said, starting another circuit round the rocking chair. 'I need to know what customers want, and where to get it from.'

Grant said, 'Your mother's suppliers will not desert you. They'll soon be in touch.'

'You're right, Inspector, I suppose.'

'I understand that you've been away some time and that you only returned yesterday.'

'Yes. I had not been getting on very well with my mother. She kept picking on me. I could never do anything right. So I left home to try to get on my feet. It was much more difficult than expected. Because I *hadn't* got a job, I couldn't *get* a job. Also, because I had left home, I couldn't give a permanent address. I didn't know it could be so tough.'

'So how long were you away, and where did you actually go?'

'I was away eight months. I went all over the place. It was the same wherever I went.'

Angel frowned. 'Well, eight months. How did you manage?'

'I didn't. I finished up sleeping rough. That was awful.'

'I'm sure,' Angel said. He ran his fingers thoughtfully across his forehead. He wondered whether it was worthwhile pressing him further on his activities.

'We've nearly finished for now, Mr Grant. There's one question I must put to you. Did your mother have any enemies?'

'Well, she was pretty forthright, Inspector. I suppose over the years, she would have made a *few* enemies. Nobody could compete with the sort of tongue lashing she could dish out, particularly if she thought somebody was trying to get the better of her. But I wouldn't have thought that those sort of skirmishes would have resulted in her murder. But I think that I should tell you, Inspector, that my mother was a law unto herself. For instance, in her opinion, there was no woman good enough for me. If ever I spoke warmly about one, my mother would always decry her and run her down. I could *never* bring a girl home. She would never have had a warm or even polite reception from my mother. So I never did. In her eyes, there was no female in Bromersley, probably the whole country good enough for me. I kept telling her that the queen had got a husband, but I couldn't possibly have changed her. Consequently any courting I did had to be on the sly.'

'So you are not aware of anybody who would want to murder your mother?' Angel said.

'Definitely not.'

'Now what about your father? Was your mother divorced or was she a widow?'

'She was divorced from him. I know very little about him. Apparently she was a dancer on the stage when she was younger and she met a man, he was a singer, Philip Grant. They had a whirlwind romance, married in 1984. I was born a year after in 1985. Shortly after I was born they fell out and he left her, then she heard he had died. She told me about it. I don't ever remember seeing him.'

Angel's pen was working overtime recording the details. 'Where did he die and when?'

'Oh, about ten or fifteen years ago. I can't be sure. I think he was living in Leeds at the time he died.'

'What was his first name, and your mother's maiden name?'

'My father's name was Philip and my mother's maiden name was Hemingway.'

'Right. Thank you. And have you seen anything here now that wasn't here before you went out? Has the murderer left anything behind?'

Grant's face creased. His eyes narrowed. 'What do you mean?'

'Cigarette packet. Used tissue. Glove. Anything. It's not unusual for criminals to be sloppy.'

'I haven't noticed anything.'

'Has anything been stolen?'

Grant frowned. 'I dunno,' he said. 'I haven't had a chance to look round, have I?'

'If you notice anything unusual, don't touch it and let us know. Where did your mother keep her money?'

'The notes she kept in a big old leather wallet, which she always had with her. In the daytime it was in her overall pocket and at night it was under her pillow.'

Angel stood up. 'I'll inquire,' he said. 'Excuse me.'

He went out of the room and into the shop.

Grant heard exchanges between Angel and some others, then the detective inspector returned with a big, old, brown leather wallet. It had edges of paper money protruding through worn out cotton stitches and was held together with two wide rubber bands. He passed it over to Grant. He hesitated, then took it and looked at it as if he shouldn't be touching it.

Grant knew that Angel was watching him. He wriggled uncomfortably and licked his bottom lip. Eventually he offered the wallet back to Angel and said, 'It looks all right to me, Inspector.'

'Better look inside it, Mr Grant,' Angel said. 'Hadn't you?'

Grant wrinkled his nose. His eyebrows drew closer together. He began to bite his lip. He looked at Angel who nodded encouragingly.

Grant hesitatingly eased the two rubber bands. He pulled them off and put them on the settee.

Angel thought they were roughly cut pieces of an inner tube from a bicycle.

Then the wallet opened in Grant's lap. It was bursting with paper money, predominately twenty-pound notes, sorted into amounts of five hundred pounds held together by red elastic bands.

Angel took in the fact that there was a minimum of nine bunches of twenty-pound notes plus a few loose wraps of twenties and some ten-pound notes, in all amounting to around £5,000.

Grant stared at it.

Angel wondered what Grant was thinking. He must be pleased that there was that money to give him confidence and enable him not to worry about where his next meal was coming from and so forth, but his mother had to die for it to happen.

Grant picked up the elastic bands and rolled them round the closed wallet.

'Is it all there?' Angel said.

Grant gave a little shrug. 'I don't know how much she had, but—'

'I meant, is that all there is? Or is there somewhere else where she keeps her money?'

'Oh yes. The coins she kept in an old Nuttalls' Mintoes tin in that cupboard,' he said, pointing at the sideboard. Then he added, 'I wonder.'

He put the wallet on the settee, stood up and crossed the room. He opened one of the sideboard doors and saw the Nuttalls' Mintoes tin, took it out to the table and prised off the lid. It was almost full with bagged silver and copper. He took out a few bags and peered into the bottom of the tin. There was an amount of mixed coins. He returned the bags he had taken out.

Angel watched him.

Grant looked satisfied. 'That's all right,' he said. He replaced the lid, put the tin back in the cupboard and returned to his seat on the settee.

'She would empty the till each evening. She'd put the notes in her wallet and the loose change in the tin. If there was enough, she'd bag it up in proper bank bags, and, as much as possible, she paid the wholesalers' delivery men and travellers' with the change and kept back the notes.'

Angel nodded, then pointing to the wallet of money he said, 'You'd better take charge of that. I should pay it into your bank for safety's sake.'

Grant looked at the wallet. He'd never held that much money. A smile slowly developed.

Angel said, 'You'll have a funeral, and your accountant and probably your solicitor to pay, and you don't know what bills your mum might have left behind.'

'That's one thing I *can* be certain of, Inspector. My mother won't have left any bills unpaid. She always paid on time. That was one of her rules.'

Angel nodded and smiled. 'Right, Mr Grant, will you empty your pockets onto the table?'

Grant frowned. Then he looked up and said, 'What for?'

'You can refuse if you want to, but I would think it awfully suspicious if you weren't willing to cooperate.'

Grant's pulse began to race. His face coloured up. 'It would make me feel a suspect, Inspector. Don't tell me you think that I could have . . .' He didn't finish what he had wanted to say.

Angel said, 'You told me you were the only living relative you knew of. You also said that your mother had told you that she had left everything of hers to you. So you had the most to gain by her death.'

'I also had the most to lose,' he said quietly.

Angel heard him, pursed his lips and said, 'It's standard procedure, Mr Grant. We search all close relatives, those who live on the same premises and especially those who will inherit. You qualify on all three counts.'

Grant sighed noisily, stood up and began to empty his pockets on the table.

He took out a spotlessly clean white linen handkerchief still folded into four, a key, a packet of twenty cigarettes, a box of matches, two one-pound coins, and a receipt from Jeeves the jeweller's. Then he patted his pockets, ostensibly to check that they were all empty and sat down.

Angel looked at the contents on the table. He opened the cigarette packet and noted that it contained fourteen cigarettes, then checked the matchbox and noted that it was almost full. He shook his head. 'Is this the lot?' he said.

'Yes,' Grant said.

Angel sighed. 'Stand up,' he said.

The muscles around Grant's mouth tightened then relaxed. He slowly got to his feet.

Angel stood up and came up to him. 'Put your arms out.'

Grant grudgingly obeyed.

Angel then patted the man's chest. He appeared to find something on his right breast. Angel's face tightened. He stepped back, pointed to it and said, 'Whatever it is, take it out.'

Grant pursed his lips, then he slowly reached into his inside pocket, took out a wodge of paper money in an elastic band and dropped it onto the table.

Angel looked at it, sighed then shook his head. He resumed the search. He patted Grant's jacket pockets, his trouser and hip pockets until he was satisfied that he was not concealing anything else.

Angel wrinkled his nose. 'Right,' he said. 'Sit down.'

Grant slumped onto the settee. He ran his hand through his hair.

Angel reached out to the table for the wodge of paper money. It had a red elastic band round it, just how it was wrapped in Mrs Grant's wallet.

Angel sat down and counted the money. 'There's £370 there,' he said.

'I'd forgotten about that,' Grant said.

Angel sniffed. He then reached out for the receipt from Jeeves the jeweller's. He looked at the figure at the bottom. He turned to Grant and said, 'It says £120. You told me it was £420.'

Grant smiled. 'No, Inspector. You must have got it wrong. I said £120.'

Angel's eyebrows shot up, his jaw muscles tightened and a red mist visible only to him came up from his chest. If there was one type of person he could not stand, it was a liar. He lunged out with his leg and kicked the underside of the table. It was like a twelve-inch gun being fired.

The contents of Grant's pockets bounced on the table top.

Grant's eyes flashed. His mouth dropped open. His heart pounded away like a Salvation Army drum.

Taylor dashed in from the shop to see what had caused the noise. Everything seemed all right to him, so he went back into the shop.

'Don't lie to me, lad,' Angel bellowed. 'It won't do you any good. I've been lied to by experts and it didn't do *them* any good.'

Grant spluttered. 'I thought I had said £120, Inspector. Er . . . erm . . . sorry if you misunderstood me.'

But Angel was angry. 'I didn't misunderstand you, lad,' he roared. 'I can see exactly what happened. So let's stop playing silly buggers! You stole £500 out of your mother's wallet. Bought yourself a watch for £120, went to the hairdresser's, he charged you eight quid, and that's why you have £372 in your pocket.'

'I didn't *steal* any money, Inspector,' Grant said. 'My mother *gave* me the money.'

'Did she? Are you sure? I suppose you are going to tell me that she also gave you the cigarettes and matches?'

Grant's face changed. 'Well, yes,' he said. 'Er, well, no.'

Angel kept up the pressure. 'Don't you *know*? Which was it? Yes or no? Or don't you know the difference? You are spewing out that many lies you wouldn't know the truth if it jumped out and bit you.'

'No,' Grant said. 'I admit it. I took those. I was desperate. I had to have a fag.'

'That's better,' Angel said more equably. '*When* did you take them?'

'In the night. I woke up to go to the bathroom. I couldn't get back to sleep.'

'Where did you get them from?'

'From the shop.'

'That's better. A lot better. You see, telling the truth is far less difficult than you thought. And it's absolutely painless.'

Angel looked directly at him.

Grant looked down at his feet. His mouth was dry. He licked his lips. His heart was pounding faster and louder. He suddenly became aware that he was breathing rapidly and unevenly so he concentrated on bringing it under control.

'You see,' Angel said. 'It didn't hurt, did it?'

Grant didn't look up.

'But you had every intention of lying to her,' Angel said, 'and telling her the watch cost £420, didn't you? After all the receipt could easily be falsified. It only needed two strokes of a ball point to change the one into a four, to make the £120 into £420. Then you would have been £300 in pocket, wouldn't you?'

The muscles in Grant's jaw tightened. This was too much.

'*All right! All right!*' he yelled. 'There was no other way of getting any money of my own together. I have a life to live. I'm thirty years of age and I have nothing. I wanted something for myself for a change. But I didn't steal the £500. Ma gave me that money, voluntarily. It meant something to her to make me look smart and well off. She had bought me a gold watch for my eighteenth birthday and I had lost it in a stupid card game.'

'Are you sure?' Angel said. 'You'd better be careful from now on, lad, that you tell me the truth.'

'I *have* told you the truth.'

'You weren't very sure a minute ago, when I asked you about the cigarettes, were you?'

'Yes. I told you, I took them.'

'You *stole* them,' Angel said, 'from your *own* mother . . .'

Grant looked down. He clasped his hands together tightly. He sniffed and went up to his top pocket for his handkerchief. It wasn't there. It was on the table. He reached out for it. Shook it open and wiped his nose. Then nasally he muttered something.

Angel said, 'What's that, Mr Grant? You said something.'

Grant looked up briefly. His face was red. He wiped his cheeks and eyes. 'You wouldn't understand,' he said.

'I'll tell you what I *do* understand,' Angel said. 'I understand that you and your mother, after a re-union last night, had a row . . . a big row, probably about money. You didn't take kindly to being pushed around by her for the rest of your life. You went to bed, but you didn't sleep very well. The row continued this morning. You couldn't do or say anything right. You had reached your limit. You couldn't stand it anymore. You resolved to change everything. When your mother went into the shop, you got a kitchen knife, followed her in and stabbed her. Then you took out her wallet, lifted the first bundle of money to hand, which happened to be £500, replaced the wallet, looked round for something to hide the stab wounds, threw a cauliflower at her and left.'

Grant gasped and briefly closed his eyes. 'It's not true,' he said. 'Not one word of it. I'm not a thief or a murderer.'

Angel's eyebrows shot up. He shook his head. 'You stole the cigarettes and matches from her. You intended relieving her of a further £300. Those are not actions of a devoted son, are they?'

Grant sent Angel a long, pained look and then broke eye contact. He swallowed hard.

'You would've had to have lived with her to understand,' he said. 'I mean, she wasn't the usual type of mother that doted on her children. Her attitude was that kids were useful to run errands and do jobs for them. Which I have always done, and then she regarded me as her insurance against loneliness in her old age. She *said* that to me.'

'You said that she wanted you to look smart and well off. That's why she wanted you to have a good watch.'

'That's also true.'

Angel wrinkled his brow, put his tongue in his cheek then said, 'You know, lad, you're going to have to make it clear to me, what part of what you say is true and what part isn't.'

Angel then looked at his watch. He stood up, turned to Grant and said, 'Excuse me. There is something I must do. We will talk again tomorrow. Please stay there a minute. One of my colleagues may be able to take your fingerprints now. It is—'

Grant eyes flashed in horror. '*My* fingerprints?' he said. 'I haven't done anything wrong.'

'It is purely for elimination, Mr Grant. That's all.'

Grant sighed. He ran his hand through his hair. 'Whenever you like, Inspector,' he said. 'I'm not going anywhere.'

Angel went out of the kitchen and into the shop to find out how far SOCO had reached.

Taylor said, 'We've completed the scene, sir. And we've been through the rubbish box in the shop, the waste bin in the kitchen and the wheelie outside. Nothing interesting, sir.'

Angel wasn't pleased. He breathed in noisily.

'We've not done the fingertip search of the house and shop yet, sir,' Taylor said.

'Right, Don,' Angel said. 'We'll sort that out tomorrow. I've finished with Grant, for the time being,' he said. 'I've left him in the kitchen. If you have a spare pair of hands, take his prints.'

'Right, sir.'

THREE

Angel came out of the little shop. He intended making for his car for some peace and quiet in order to think things out. But there was a gathering of eight or so women on the pavement in front of the shop window. When they saw Angel they advanced towards him. A rough-looking woman said, 'Are you in charge of this case, young man?'

'Yes, madam,' Angel said. 'Why?'

'Well, what's happened to Gladys Grant, and how long are we going to have to wait to get into the shop? There are things we need. We have all got to feed our kids and our men folk, you know.'

Some of the rest of the group muttered their agreement and pressed forward, surrounding him.

Angel wrinkled his nose. He needed to think out what to say.

The policeman on the door came up to them. Angel caught his eye and with an easy look, assured him that he did not need any assistance.

Angel said, 'Well, tragically, early this morning, somebody came into the shop and murdered Mrs Grant.'

The women were aghast.

'Oh my god,' one of them said.

'Poor sod,' said another.

'I told you,' said a third.

And a fourth said, 'Oh, how awful.'

'If anybody knows anything or saw a person entering or leaving the shop early this morning, they should tell me about it.'

The gathering of people looked at each other then back at Angel. 'None of us saw anything, sorry. When will the shop be open?'

'I don't know, but we will be leaving shortly. I don't know whether Mr Grant will want to open up or what will happen. That's up to him. I'm sorry.'

Angel turned away from the gathering, intent on leaving the scene to return to the office when he saw a big yellow van pull up close behind his BMW. Angel realized it was a bread van. A man dressed in a white coat and hat got out. The driver went to the back of the van and began sorting out a wooden tray and was filling it with bread and cakes in accordance with a book he was holding. Angel went up to him.

'Excuse me,' he said, taking out his ID and showing it to the man.

The bread man glanced up casually from the order book. 'Yes?' he said. When he saw Angel's ID, he lowered the book and gave the inspector his full attention. 'Police?' he said.

'I'm afraid you won't be able to deliver anything to Grant's today. There's a serious incident being looked into.'

The delivery man smiled confidently. 'That's all right,' he said, 'Mrs Grant *ordered* this stuff.'

'I'm afraid Mrs Grant is dead.'

The bread man stood motionless for several seconds, then he said, 'What happened? She was as right as rain yesterday.'

'What time was that?'

'About five o'clock. I popped in about then. I only live round the corner on Fountain Street. I actually pass here on my way to work.'

'What time was that?'

'Well, I start at 8, but I was a bit late so I reckon it would be just after eight this morning.'

'Were you on foot?'

'No, I was in my car, and, as a matter of fact, I saw an old woman with grey hair in a long sheepskin coat go into the shop.'

Angel's eyebrows went up. His chest began to burn. 'Are you sure?'

'Yes. Positive,' he said. 'Poor old Cliff, her son, you know. How's he taken it?'

'Pretty well, I think. Look, we will need you to make a formal statement. What's your name?'

He reached into his top pocket and pulled out a card with the baker's name and address on it, and his name across the middle. 'Maddison, Percy Maddison. Of course, anything I can do to help. How awful. Give my condolences to Cliff, will you, Inspector?'

Angel nodded. The man shoved the tray of bread and cakes back into the van and quickly drove away.

Angel made for his car. He was in a buoyant mood;. he was thinking it was good to have an eyewitness for a change. Closing the car door, he reached into his pocket, pulled out his mobile and phoned the mortuary. He managed eventually to speak to Dr Mac.

'You disappeared before I had the opportunity to have a word with you,' Angel said.

'I looked into the room where you were, Michael,' Mac said. 'You were interviewing somebody. I didn't think you'd welcome an interruption.'

It was true. 'Yeah. Yeah,' he said. 'Well, anyway, what you got?'

'I haven't had chance to look at her yet. Should get to her tomorrow. What I can tell you from the in-situ examination, is that she died from three knife wounds to the heart, and that she died between five and eight o'clock this morning.'

'Thanks, Mac,' he said. 'What do you make of the cauliflower?'

'I don't make anything of it. I wouldn't think it played any part in causing her death, Michael, if that's what you're asking me. But I can't be absolutely sure. I may be able to report more *after* the post mortem.'

'Thank you, Mac,' Angel said and he ended the call. He pushed the mobile back into his pocket, reached down to the ignition switch and was about to turn the key, when the delectable DS Flora Carter tapped lightly on the car window.

He smiled when he saw her. He noticed her eyes looked brighter than usual. She was also smiling. Angel thought she looked so pleased with herself that maybe she had discovered something on the door to door. He pressed the button and lowered the window.

'Got something, Flora?'

'Yes, sir,' she said.

With a hand gesture he indicated that she should go round the car and get in.

When she had closed the door she said, 'A woman in a house only three doors up said that just after eight this morning, from her bedroom window, she saw a strange woman with grey hair, in a long sheepskin coat, walk into the shop.'

That was confirmation of what Maddison, the bread delivery man had said. A warm glow developed and expanded in Angel's chest. His hand went up to his face. He ran his fingertips up and down his temple. 'That's great, Flora. We now have *two* independent witnesses. Is that the best description you can get? I mean, is there anything more she can tell us?'

'It's the most I could get, sir,' she said. 'Would you like to speak to her yourself?'

'I would. What's her name and which house is it?'

'Mrs Rhoda Lee, 202 Canal Street.'

He scribbled it down on his notes. Then he looked up and said, 'Have you finished the door to door?'

'Yes, sir,' she said.

'Where's Trevor Crisp?'

'Haven't seen him for about an hour. He'll still be out there, on the knocker, I expect.'

Angel pursed his lips. He wished he could be sure of it. 'Right, Flora. See you tomorrow.'

Flora Carter rushed off.

He got out of his car which was parked behind the SOC van. He saw that on the pavement, by the side of the van were the four SOC men. They were taking off their white sterile disposable overalls, which had to be discarded before they arrived at the next crime scene so that there was no possibility of the cross contamination of evidence.

Angel spotted DS Taylor and went up to him. 'I see you're ready for off, Don. What have you found out that I will need to know?'

'Well, sir,' Taylor said. 'She was stabbed three times in the heart. And you know about the cauliflower. There were several grains of rice — at least I think it's rice — on her clothes, her neck and her chest. I'll be checking on them and I'll let you know.'

Angel's eyes widened, his eyebrows went up. '*Rice*?' he said. 'Where did *that* come from?'

Taylor shrugged then he said, 'Well, it is a grocer's shop. I expect she sold rice.'

Angel shook his head. He didn't think that that explained why there were grains of the stuff on her body. 'Anything else?'

'Don't think so, sir.'

'Right, Don. Thank you. .'

Angel then set off walking along Canal Street. His mind was on the rice. Several grains of rice on her clothes, her neck and her chest, Taylor had said. Angel tried to dredge up from his memory what he knew about rice. It was a staple food and was grown in China and India and parts of Asia. So what? It was sometimes used as confetti at weddings. Much more frequently, it had milk added, was cooked in an oven and served as a pudding. His mother had made hundreds of them in her lifetime, and Mary had made a few. Lately, Mary had also been serving up chicken with rice and vegetables and calling it 'chicken risotto'. But he had wandered a little way from the point. Why were there grains of rice on Gladys Grant's body? He had to find out if the rice was cooked and left to go cold, or if it was in its dry state. It would not matter, but then again, it might. Mac would be able to advise him further on the subject.

A raucous horn blast from a passing car brought him back to realize where he was. He was walking down Canal Street. He was looking for house number 202. He looked up at the doors. There it was. He knocked on the door.

A middle-aged woman with a cigarette hanging from the corner of her mouth opened it.

'What do you want, love?' she said with a wrinkled brow and wiping her hands on a towel as she spoke.

'Mrs Rhoda Lee?' he said.

'Yes,' she said. 'You a copper?'

Angel nodded.

She stepped back and opened the door wider. 'It's really awful about Gladys Grant,' she said. 'Mindst you, she could be a bit sharp if she wasn't getting her own way, you know. And it doesn't do to make enemies, especially when you're in business. Well, come in. Come in. Don't stand out there.'

'Thank you,' he said. He was in a small sitting room.

'Sit yourself down, we're not posh, but it's all paid for,' she said with a smile.

Angel removed his hat and nodded his understanding.

'You told my sergeant that you saw a woman walk into Grant's shop early this morning?' he said.

'Yes. A grey-haired woman.'

'How old do you reckon she was?'

She frowned. 'Dunno. Hard to say. I mean, she was no lightweight flighty lass in her teens or her twenties. At the same time, she was no old biddy. But she was very odd-looking.'

Angel pursed his lips. 'How do you mean, odd-looking?'

'I don't know. I meant odd-looking. Peculiar like. I can't put it into words. Maybe she wasn't the full shilling.'

Angel blinked and rubbed his chin.

'Was she the murderer then?' Rhoda Lee said. 'It would be a funny sort of justice if it was a woman that did her in, wouldn't it?'

'Why do you say that?'

'Well, I know you shouldn't speak ill of the dead, but Gladys Grant had a wicked, unforgiving tongue on her, and a memory longer than a dole queue.'

'She made a lot of enemies?'

'Not enemies exactly. I just mean she wasn't at all popular. She always spoke her piece when it would have been kinder sometimes to have kept her mouth shut.'

He nodded knowingly. 'That woman you saw this morning . . . you said she had *grey* hair?' he said. 'Was it long and flowing grey hair, or curled up tight or in a bun?'

'It was curled up tight, as you call it, I think. And she was wearing a long sheepskin coat.'

'What were her shoes like?'

'Didn't notice, to tell the truth.'

'Was she wearing a skirt or trousers?'

'I don't know. I only saw her for a few moments. I've told you and that other female copper all I know.'

'Was she carrying anything?'

'I don't know. She had a hand up her front. I suppose she could have had summat in it.'

'Which direction did she come from?'

'Looked like she had come from the direction of the main road, and walked straight from there all the way along Canal Street. And don't ask me which way she went when she came out because I wasn't there to see her.'

'And what time was this?'

'A couple of minutes past eight.'

'How can you be so sure about the time?'

'My alarm goes at eight o'clock, and I always get out of bed promptly. If I didn't, I might fall back to sleep again, and that would never do. I did that once and didn't wake up until half past eleven. No. The alarm went. I got out of bed and crossed to the window to see what sort of a morning it was, and that's when I seed her. And that would be a minute or two past eight.'

'Thank you, Mrs Lee. You've been most helpful.' He turned towards the door.

'Do you know who done it then?' she said.

He looked back at her and said, 'We're working on it, Mrs Lee.'

He made a quick exit and proceeded back to his car. It had been a long, hard day. He let in the clutch and pointed the car bonnet home. He looked at his watch. He sighed heavily. He was going to be late. Mary would not be pleased. Particularly as it was her shopping evening. Most shops in Bromersley were kept open an extra two hours or so on Tuesday, and as a matter of interest to him, he was in need of a haircut, and he had to find a present to celebrate his and Mary's twenty-fifth wedding anniversary, coming up in nine days' time, on 14 May, and he had it in mind secretly to buy Mary something special to celebrate the occasion.

It was 6.30 p.m. on the same day, Tuesday 5 May 2015 in the town centre of Bromersley. A strong wind was building up to a gale. Trees were waving and bending precariously over the roads, railways and houses. The sky was filled with black clouds. More heavy rain was imminent. Tired and irritable shoppers with their umbrellas were pushing through the wind to their cars, the bus stop or round the sweaty stalls in the market. Weary vendors were looking with disdain at the clock while thinking about the amount of unsold stock they were going to be humping back home. Every person was in a hurry to get somewhere but nobody was seen to arrive, and everybody was impatient.

As it happened, Mary was in Cheapo's supermarket, looking for the latest bargains, where Angel had dropped her while he called at the hairdresser's for a short back and sides.

Next door was Ashton's antique shop. Daniel Ashton had been in CID a few years ago. He had left the police to take over his father's small antique shop in town. Angel called in briefly to keep in touch with his long-standing old friend. In addition, he also wanted to see if Ashton had any special piece of jewellery that he thought Mary would like for their anniversary.

'What's your budget, Michael?' Daniel Ashton said.

'Well,' Angel said, rubbing his chin. 'I reckon I could go to £500 if it was *really* exceptional. But it would *have* to be exceptional.'

Ashton turned away from the safe and brought a small, black display pad with eight rings in it. 'Your twenty-fifth, you said? Well, there's a lovely ruby and diamond ring, I could do it for £450, but that would really be for a ruby wedding.'

Angel looked at the label. It was marked £595. He thought Daniel was offering him a good price, but as he said, the ruby ring was for forty years of married bliss and he couldn't yet claim that.

On the same pad was a sparkling, large single stone ring twinkling away at him. Daniel kept moving the box slightly so that the stones in the rings caught the light.

Angel replaced the ruby and diamond and picked up the sparkler. 'How much is this, Daniel?' he said.

'That's too much for you, Michael. It's way out of your budget. It's great value. It's £900. It's a diamond solitaire in platinum. White as snow.'

Angel took it to the sunlight coming through the glass window in the door. Without magnification the stone looked clean, it was claw set and there was no illusion setting around the stone to make it look bigger than it really was. It looked very good. Very good indeed. He tried it on his little finger up to the first joint, which he knew was the size of Mary's third finger of her left hand. It fitted a treat. He returned to the counter and handed it back to Ashton.

'What could you do that for?' Angel said.

Ashton pulled a few faces, and ran a hand across his mouth and chin. 'I can't get anywhere near £500, Michael,' he said. He blew out a long breath heavily, had another look at it and said, 'I haven't much margin on it. The best I could do would be £800.'

Angel's nose went up. It was beyond him. 'Eight hundred pounds,' he said. He nodded, pursed his lips and looked down. Then he looked up and said, 'Well, thanks very much, Daniel. Have you anything else?'

'Not in the jewellery line, Michael,' he said. 'Keep popping in. I might get something in that you like. How is the lovely Mary, by the way?'

'Oh, she's fine,' Angel said.

Ashton smiled. 'You were lucky to get her, you know. I dated her twice, but she didn't really want me.'

It was Angel's turn to smile.

'How's work?' Ashton said. 'I see you soon cleared up the murder of that actress, Joan Minter. Are you on a murder at the moment?'

'Yes,' Angel said and he quickly told him the basic facts about the Gladys Grant case.

Then he took his leave and drove the BMW onto Cheapo's car park to collect Mary as arranged. He had to put on the car sidelights as it was getting gloomy due to the dark clouds and the rain. The car park was packed with cars and vans. He eventually found a place and parked the car there. The rain was coming down from every direction due to the powerful wind that was howling like a dog. As he pulled on the handbrake, at the other side of the car park, he saw an elderly lady struggling to pack groceries into the back of her car. Then suddenly, apparently without her realizing it, a can or a tin fell out of the old lady's car onto the tarmac.

Angel switched the windscreen wipers back on so that he could see better.

Being on a slight slope, the can began to roll away from her. A young tall man appeared from somewhere, chased after the tin, stopped it and picked it up. The rain was exceptionally heavy at that time. The young man had no hat or umbrella. Angel thought the tin was a can of Monty's lager, a heavily advertised brand being trialled in South Yorkshire.

He ran back with the tin to the old lady to return it to her. She was protected from the downpour somewhat by being under the tailgate of her car. At first, when she looked at the tin she seemed to hesitate as if she doubted that it belonged to her. The man appeared to have to explain. Eventually she opened up a shopping bag and the man dropped it in. The young man then quickly disappeared among the many cars and vans on the car park.

Angel pursed his lips, deliberated and was cheered when he considered that true chivalry in Bromersley was not dead after all.

Then he saw his wife at the store entrance holding a plastic shopping bag. She was looking round for him. He quickly got out of the car and waved to her. She saw him and waved back. He had to hold onto his hat. He quickly crossed the busy car park towards her.

'There you are,' he said with a smile.

He held his hand out for the shopping bag.

She gave it to him. 'Thank you, darling,' she said.

He guided her into the car, closed the door and got in himself.

Then, when they were out of the downpour, he wrinkled his nose and peered into the shopping bag. 'What's in here?' he asked. 'Something for tea?'

FOUR

It was 8.28 a.m. the following morning, Wednesday, 6 May.

Angel dashed into his office to see if anything important or urgent had come in. There seemed to be nothing on his desk that couldn't wait.

The phone rang. He reached out for it. 'Angel,' he said.

A well-spoken genteel voice he rarely heard said, 'This is Mrs Kenworthy, Inspector Angel.'

She was the Chief Constable's secretary. She knew everything that was going on in the station before anybody else and was carefully listened to when she spoke.

Angel put on his best Sunday manner and said, 'Good morning, Mrs Kenworthy, and what can I do for you this beautiful spring morning?'

'Well, Inspector,' she said. 'It's regarding your application to see the Chief Constable. You may know that he is attending an Interpol conference in Florence later this week?'

'Yes,' he said, which wasn't the truth at all, but he thought it might speed things along if he simply answered in the affirmative.

'Well, of course he is exceedingly busy preparing for it, but he has a window later this morning at 9.15, if that is convenient to you. I know it's very short notice.'

'That's fine,' Angel said.

If the Chief Constable wants to see you, he *always* dictates the time and place. His secretary was merely going through the motions. If the big cheese has a window open, better close it for him quick, before he catches pneumonia.

'I will be there, Mrs Kenworthy. Thank you. Goodbye.' He replaced the receiver, noted the appointment in his desk diary, and tried to remember what he was doing before the phone rang.

There was a knock at the door.

'Come in,' Angel said.

It was Detective Constable Ahmed Ahaz from Bromersley CID.

Ahmed was Angel's right-hand man. He considered him to be keen, industrious and thoroughly reliable.

'I saw you come in, sir,' he said.

Angel nodded. 'Anything happen here yesterday that's important, Ahmed?' he said.

'No, sir. A couple of cases of house-breaking, and a domestic. That's all.'

Angel blinked. That was unusually quiet, he was thinking, when the phone rang. He reached out for it.

'Angel,' he said.

He could hear heavy, laboured breathing from the earpiece. He knew it was Superintendent Harker.

'Ah, Angel,' Harker said. 'There's been a triple nine from a woman in a flat just behind the Civic Centre. Flat 22, Monserrat House, Monserrat Street.'

'I know it, sir,' Angel said. 'It's round the corner from Canal Street.'

'The caller said that her friend, Fay Hough, is dead. Call timed in at 0830 hours. Control has sent a patrol car to secure the scene. The rest I'll leave with you.'

'Who reported it, sir?'

'The victim's friend, a Mrs Ivory,' Harker said then the line went dead. He had terminated the call.

Angel looked up at Ahmed. 'Another suspected murder,' Angel said as he scribbled the address on the back of a used envelope. He passed it to him. 'Here,' Angel said. 'Inform Dr Mac. He'll know what to do. And ask Inspector Asquith if he'll organize security there until further notice. Do that on the CID phone then come back, will you?'

Ahmed nodded. 'Right, sir,' he said and he was gone.

Angel picked up the phone and tapped out the SOCO number. Don Taylor answered. Angel told him of the situation and gave him the address. 'You'd finished at Grant's shop anyway, hadn't you?' he said.

'No, sir,' Taylor said. 'We haven't done the search of the house and shop.'

Angel pursed his lips. 'I'll see to that,' he said. 'You get out to Monserrat House ASAP. I'll see you there later.'

Then he ended the call and immediately tapped in another number.

'Yes, sir?' It was DS Flora Carter.

Angel told her about the body at Monserrat Flats and gave her the address. Then he said, 'Have you seen Trevor Crisp?'

'No, sir. He's probably still on the door to door around the Grant murder.'

'Right,' he said. 'I want you to find him and assist him, if necessary, to finish those off, then both of you go to Monserrat and begin the door to door there. They will all be flats. Just do the flats on the same floor.'

'Right, sir,' she said and he replaced the phone.

Angel pushed back the swivel chair, leaned back and sighed. Then he rubbed his chin and wondered who or what he might have missed.

There was a knock at the door.

'Come in,' he called.

It was Ahmed. 'That's all OK, sir.'

'Great stuff,' Angel said. 'Now I want DC Scrivens, ASAP, Ahmed. Find him for me, will you, lad?'

'He *was* in CID, sir. I'll see if he's still there.'

Angel came out of the Chief Constable's office on the top floor of the police station. He seemed to be pleased with the outcome and as he made his way down the stairs to the ground floor, he found himself subconsciously singing 'I feel pretty' from West Side Story. He received a strange look from a young civilian girl from the general office, who was coming up the stairs. That made him think about the words he was singing, which resulted in him stopping the singing abruptly.

He peered into CID, saw DC Scrivens, and said, 'Ted, I want you to accompany me to Grant's house and shop to search the place. Are you busy with anything that can't wait?'

'No, sir,' the young man said.

'Right. We'll go in my car.'

Five minutes later, they arrived in the BMW outside Grant's shop on Sebastopol Terrace.

The shop customers and curiosity mongers had dwindled away. The street was deserted. There were no other cars or vehicles around. Angel was pleased to see that the sign in the window of the shop door indicated that the shop was open.

Angel and Scrivens went into the shop. The shop bell peeled out its loud ringing. Angel went through the door in the counter and Scrivens followed. When they arrived in the little living room, they saw Cliff Grant laid on the settee. He had his eyes closed. He was dressed, except for his shoes, and was wearing the blue smock his mother used to wear in the shop. His eyes opened.

'I thought I heard the shop bell,' he said. 'Was it you, Inspector?'

Angel nodded and smiled.

'I was just resting my eyes,' Grant said. 'That shop bell hasn't stopped ringing since eight o'clock this morning. Everybody asking me about my mother. And wanting to buy stuff. And I don't know where anything is, and I don't know the price of it. I've just had to guess.'

Grant saw Scrivens for the first time. 'Who is this?'

Angel said, 'This is a colleague of mine.'

Grant's eyebrows shot up. He sat up on the settee, swivelled round and put his feet into his slippers strategically positioned on the floor. 'What do you want?' he said. 'I thought you had finished here yesterday.'

'We have come to search the property, Mr Grant,' Angel said.

Grant pulled his head back in surprise. 'What for?'

'Standard procedure in a murder case,' Angel said. 'We won't have finished here until we find out who murdered your mother.'

The shop bell went.

Grant stood up and made for the shop. 'Well, if you must, I suppose you must.'

He went out.

Angel turned to Scrivens. 'You start upstairs. You know what we're looking for, the usual things, gold bullion, diamonds or precious stones, unusually large quantity of jewellery, drugs, cash, any items that look as if they might be the proceeds of a robbery or a forgery, and, in this instance, any quantity of cauliflowers and rice.'

Scrivens frowned. 'Cauliflowers and rice, sir?'

83 Sebastopol Terrace was only a small house so Angel didn't expect it to take long for the two of them to carry out a search. They made a thorough job of it. They looked in the loft above the landing, and in the old coalhouse outside the back door. They checked all the room floors. Where any floor boards were loose, they were taken up, underneath was searched and the boards were replaced. In the tiny bathroom, the bath was boxed in. Scrivens carefully removed the hardboard panel from the long side and, crouching on the floor, looked at the farthest reaches of it with a torch, but there was nothing.

The shop bell rang occasionally, which kept Grant off the settee some of the time. As Angel searched the shop itself, he noticed that Grant had a pleasant repartee with the customers, most of whom he had grown up with and knew him well enough to call him Cliff. Also, he noticed that with his good looks and personal charm to a certain age group of women and girls, if he didn't have the item in the shop that they had asked for, he was able sometimes to woo them into buying an alternative item that was already in stock.

Angel saw that there was a fair sprinkling of rice on the clean, linoleum covered floor around and underneath the place where the body of Gladys Grant had been found.

In a quiet moment when there weren't any customers, Angel turned to Grant and said, 'Is the shop floor usually like this?'

Grant looked down at the sprinkling of rice. 'It's usually clean enough to eat off, Inspector,' he said. 'But I haven't had time. Ma would have swept that up straight after it happened.'

Angel nodded. He was sure that was the case. *His* mother would have done exactly the same.

'Where are the packets of rice?' he said.

Grant's eyebrows knitted together. 'I don't know if we have any. I've seen tinned rice pudding somewhere, but not dry like that.'

They scoured the stock round and about the tiny shop. After a few minutes, Grant said, 'No, Inspector. I don't think we have any. And I've not been asked for it since . . . since . . . erm, since I came back.'

'And cauliflowers, did your mum stock cauliflowers?'

'Shouldn't think so, Inspector,' Grant said. 'At least, not on a regular basis. You see, this tiny shop is only for the convenience of its customers. I recognize that. I shouldn't think any of our customers bought the bulk of their weekly grocery needs from my mother. This shop is to top up what they forgot, or what they've run out of, or what they didn't want to hump from the supermarket, or what they suddenly have a fancy for. They look on the shop as an extension of their own larders. Ma would never have thought she could possibly have competed with Cheapo's on the vast range they have as well as the price. But she's only round the corner for a couple of hundred households, is most likely open when the whim takes the householder, and she doesn't have to spend a lot at a time walking up and down aisles and queuing at cash tills.'

Angel understood only too well and he continued looking behind a pile of boxes of breakfast cereals.

At 11.30, Angel and Scrivens had finished the search. Neither of them had found anything incriminating. They hadn't found anything that might have been illegal and might have led to a prosecution of any kind, nor any dried rice nor cauliflower, nor anything that would have assisted with the investigation into Gladys Grant's murder. Angel wasn't pleased. But he was satisfied that they had been thorough and that nothing had been overlooked.

Angel and Scrivens came together in the sitting room.

Angel's mobile began to ring. It was Mac. It must be important. He almost never phoned Angel. He preferred to communicate by email.

He reached into his pocket. He opened the phone. Angel put it to his ear. 'What is it, Mac?'

'Michael!' the Glaswegian said. 'I'm at this crime scene at Monserrat House. And I've uncovered some very interesting facts you'll want to know about.'

Angel blinked. He noticed that Mac sounded breathless. Angel thought he must be excited about something. It was unusual for him to become animated about the discovery of anything in his capacity of pathologist.

'What's that, Mac?' Angel said.

'There are too many similarities for it to be coincidental.'

'Spit it out, Mac. What are you talking about?'

'This body, here at Monserrat House, a Mrs Fay Hough. Do you know that she has three stab wounds in the heart, a cauliflower in her lap and a few grains of rice on her chest?'

Angel's jaw dropped open. He squeezed his eyes shut.

'Are you there, Michael?' the doctor said.

'I'm here, Mac. I'm here,' he said. 'I heard you. I was thinking.'

'Aye. I can believe that,' Mac said. 'There's something else.'

'What's that?'

'I've found a note. It's from the murderer. Handwritten. Sticking out of her nightdress.'

Angel's heart began to beat faster. 'A note?'

'Aye. That's what I said.'

Angel sighed.

'Shall I read it to you?' Mac said.

Angel was thinking. He knew that murderers who leave notes for the investigator are usually psychopaths, who kill because they like killing, and are always difficult to fathom because they are so unpredictable.

Angel breathed out a long breath and said, 'I'll come straight over.'

Monserrat House was only two minutes in a car from Sebastopol Terrace.

Angel stopped the BMW at the foot of the off-white twelve storey high block that had been built in 1960, supposedly to abolish the pressing housing shortage in Bromersley. He went into the lobby, entered the lift and pressed the button. The lift cage glided silently up to the second floor. Almost opposite the lift doors was a uniformed constable standing outside the door of a flat.

The constable saluted him. Angel went up to him, acknowledged the salute and said, 'Good afternoon, Constable. Is this flat 22?'

'It is, sir.'

'Who is in there?'

'Dr Mac, DS Taylor and three other SOCOs, sir,' he said.

Angel nodded. 'Thank you,' he said. Then he pressed the door handle down and the door opened. He noticed the crowbar marks on the door itself, and on the door jamb both above and below the lock, it was clear to see how access to the flat had been made.

Angel went inside. The door opened straight into a big room, with big windows. It had a table in the centre of the room with six dining chairs neatly tucked underneath. There were several easy chairs, a settee and a television.

Don Taylor came up to him in his white sterile overalls, holding a clipboard.

Dr Mac was standing at the entrance to a room with his bag in his hand. He looked as if he was about to leave. He had discarded his whites, and changed out of his boots back to shoes.

Angel looked quickly from one to the other, finally settling on the doctor. 'Right, Mac. Let's see the note.'

The doctor said, 'I haven't got it, Michael. Don has it.' He pointed to DS Taylor.

Taylor said, 'I've got it here, sir.'

Wearing white, skin tight rubber gloves, he unzipped a white sterile bag which was on the dining table and took out a small, clear plastic box, removed the lid and inside was a much folded sheet of A4 paper. In the folded state, the paper measured 11¾" by ¾".

'One end of this fold was sticking out of her nightdress, at the neck,' Dr Mac said. 'If it hadn't been sticking out, I probably wouldn't have found it until the post mortem.'

Angel nodded.

Taylor reached out for two pairs of tweezers. By use of them he unfolded the paper to reveal the message. He held the paper out for the inspector to see.

Angel saw that it was neatly printed by hand in black on plain white paper.

He read it aloud:

Fay Hough was very self-willed,

She got her own way and had to be killed.

Fay is the second, there are four more to go.

Mac said, 'I think it's supposed to be poetry, if it is, it's nae like Robbie Burns.'

Angel rubbed his chin. He turned to Taylor and said, 'I want that photocopied, Don. Make three copies. Email one to the graphologist. See what he makes of it.'

'Right, sir,' Taylor said.

'I don't like that line that says Fay is the second, and that there are *four* more to go.'

Taylor said, 'It suggests we've got a serial killer on our hands, sir.'

Angel nodded. 'And all the signs are that she is a psychopath,' he said. 'So we are going to have to be especially careful and thorough. It seems that our psychopath is so confident that she dares to give advance notice of her intention to murder *four* more.'

'Are you sure it's a woman, sir?'

Angel said, 'No, I'm not, but a woman was seen entering the shop at the critical time in the Gladys Grant case by two independent witnesses. On present showing, this looks like the work of the same crazy female, doesn't it?'

Taylor nodded. 'But stabbing is predominantly a male method of committing murder.'

'True, but it doesn't entirely preclude women,' Angel said. 'There have been plenty of instances where a woman has used a dagger or a stiletto.' He then turned to the doctor. 'You might very well find a similar verse of poetry on Gladys Grant's body, Mac.'

The doctor frowned. 'I might very well, Michael.'

Angel's forehead creased. 'If you do, or if you don't, I'd like to know about it, Mac, ASAP.'

'Aye, Michael. I'll check up on it as soon as I get back there.' Then he said, 'Anyhow, will you take a good look at this poor woman so that I can get her moved?'

He nodded. 'Where is she?' he said.

'In the bedroom, sir,' Taylor said. 'Through this door. Follow me.'

Angel entered the bedroom, stopped and looked round. One of the two SOCOs there was taking photographs, the other was checking off a list from a clipboard. The room was generally tidy and clean. He looked at the double bed. It had obviously been slept in, by one person. The duvet was neatly turned back from a top corner and there was a dent in the pillow where a head had been.

Taylor went round to the other side of the bed. Angel followed him. And there it was.

On the carpeted floor leaning against a bedside table was the body of a woman aged about sixty, in a nightdress, housecoat and slippers. The heart and stomach area was covered in ruddy brown dried blood, and in her lap was a blood-spattered cauliflower.

The muscles of Angel's jaw tightened. His heart beat faster.

He approached the body and leaned over it. He saw small white flecks — he thought to be rice — on her neck, around her body and on the carpet. He counted them. They added up to twenty-four.

He straightened up, stepped back a pace and rubbed his chin. He then turned to the doctor and said, 'Have you got a time of death for this, Mac?'

'Aye. It's looking like sometime between five o'clock and eight o'clock, this morning.'

Angel's eyes narrowed. 'Same as Gladys Grant.'

The doctor said, 'Can I have the body now, Michael?'

'Poor woman. I've seen all I need to see. Yes, Mac, of course. As soon as you like.'

'Ah,' Mac said. He opened his phone and scrolled down for a number.

Angel turned to Taylor. 'Was this lady, Fay Hough, married?'

'Yes. I understand from her friend and neighbour that she was.'

Angel said, 'Well, the husband should be told as a matter of great urgency. Who is this neighbour? I'd better see her.'

'It's the lady who found her, sir. Her name is Mrs Ivory.'

Angel nodded and turned towards the bedroom door. 'I'll see her now, if I can.'

Taylor said, 'She lives a couple of doors away. Flat 24.'

FIVE

Angel knocked on the door of Flat 24 Monserrat House and waited.

The door was opened by a slim, pretty lady. Her face was bright pink, her cheeks a little puffed and her eyes were red. She was holding a tissue.

Angel could see that she had been crying. 'I'm sorry to bother you,' he said. 'I'm from Bromersley Police. Are you Mrs Ivory?'

She stepped back and opened the door more widely. 'Yes, I am,' she said. 'Please come in.'

She showed him into the sitting room. 'Please sit down.'

'Thank you,' he said. 'I'm Detective Inspector Angel.'

She smiled weakly and said, 'Yes, I know.'

He looked at her closely. 'Have we met before?'

'I've seen your picture in the papers and on the television often enough to remember,' she said. 'You're the one who *always* gets his man, like the Mounties, aren't you?'

The muscles of his face tightened then relaxed. Whenever anyone said that he always got his man, it worried him that it might be the very next murder case he was investigating when he didn't.

'My team and I always do our very best, Mrs Ivory,' he said quickly to get it out of the way. Then he said, 'I understand that you found the body of Mrs Hough earlier this morning? Would you tell me about it?'

The corners of her mouth turned down. 'Oh dear,' she said. 'Yes, of course.'

Angel took the envelope out of his inside pocket and began to make notes.

Mrs Ivory said, 'Well, Fay and I have been friends for many years, and when my husband died last year, she and her husband became even closer friends of mine. And one of the things Fay and I did together was go to the gym. Now we found that going early in the morning was the best time to go because it wasn't as busy. So as Lance was away — Lance is Fay's husband — we had arranged to go to the gym *this* morning, and I was to collect her as soon as I was ready after quarter past eight. This morning I was on time. I knocked on her door. When I didn't get any reply, I tried it, found it was unlocked, came in and called out. Of course, there was no reply. It seemed strange. I walked through the flat, calling all the time so that I wouldn't surprise her. I went into the kitchen, the bathroom and I went into the bedroom last of all and . . . and . . . and found her . . .'

Her voice trailed away. She dabbed her eyes with the tissue.

Angel put down the ballpoint, looked across at her and said, 'I'm sorry.' Then he waited a moment and said, 'But I have to ask . . . what did you do next?'

'I didn't touch her,' she said. 'It wasn't necessary. I rushed out of the flat back into here. Then I picked up the phone and dialled 999.'

'Did you touch anything in the flat?'

'No,' she said. 'At least I don't think so. Maybe the door handles. I am not sure.'

'Do you know of any person who might have wanted to murder Mrs Hough?'

'Certainly not. Lance and Fay Hough are the nicest couple anybody would like to have met.'

'Where is Mr Hough right now?'

'I don't know precisely, Inspector. Fay would have known, of course. I know he is away on business. He is sometimes away. He is in management at Mixendon's Glass Works on Wells Road. They will know.'

He made a note of it, then looked up at her and smiled. 'Do you happen to know if anything is missing from the flat?'

She shook her head. 'I don't know.'

He persisted. 'Did they have any valuables . . . gold, silver, any cash in the flat? Any antiques?'

'Not as far as I know.'

He rubbed his chin.

Then his phone rang. 'Excuse me, Mrs Ivory,' he said, and he pulled his mobile out of his pocket. He looked at the LCD screen. It was Mac. It must be important. He almost never phoned Angel. He preferred to communicate by email. Angel stood up and turned away from Mrs Ivory.

He pressed the button. 'Yes, Mac?'

'Ah, Michael. You wanted to know if there was a note on Gladys Grant's body?'

'I certainly do.'

'The answer to that one is yes. At least, there's a sheet of paper, same size and folded like the other one and sticking out of her bra. Do you want me to open it up and read it to you?'

Angel interpreted that as confirmation that it was a serial killer he was after. He felt as if he had a hot brick inside his chest. His heart beat was stronger. He positively *ached* for a clue to the killer.

'No. Keep it as it is, Mac.'

'Right. There's something else, Michael,' the doctor said. 'It's about the rice — and I can confirm that it *is* dried rice all right. On examination firstly of Gladys Grant, I discovered that her mouth was filled to bursting with grains of rice, so I naturally immediately checked the mouth of Fay

Hough. And I discovered that her mouth was also filled with rice. However, the rice didn't have anything to do with their deaths. It had been deliberately put into their mouths *post* mortem. I assume it was put there by the murderer. I canna say that I can understand it, Michael.'

Angel rang the mortuary bell.

The door was opened by a man in a green operating gown, green trousers and white wellington boots. Angel knew him from his many visits to the mortuary over the years.

'Hello, Inspector. Come in. You want to see Dr Mac, I take it?'

'Yes, John. He *is* expecting me.'

'He is working on one of yours now, I think, in the operating theatre. You know your way? Straight through that door, Inspector.'

'Thank you, John,' Angel said and he pushed open the door.

The theatre was a big white tiled room. There was the bank of refrigerated drawers, like forty giant filing cabinet drawers down one wall. There were four operating tables. Two of them had a covered cadaver on them.

The stench was unbelievable. It was the result of the opening of human innards, and it competed with the alternative acrid smell of ammonia. At that moment the former was winning. In the background, there was the perpetual humming of the refrigerator compressor, together with the clatter and vibration of the bank of cold metal drawers it served.

Angel was not unfamiliar with the environment.

Dr Mac was in a green operating gown with wellington boots. He was leaning over a body on one of the operating tables. The body was covered with white waterproof covers, leaving open only the area around the heart where he had been working. There was a large powerful lamp overhead.

Beyond, another man in green was wielding a hose pipe and flushing the tiled walls and floor. There was a network of narrow channels across the floor of the room for water and human waste to drain away.

Mac sensed that someone had entered. He turned. He had a scalpel in one rubber covered hand and a swab in the other, and he had a powerful extra lens attached to his spectacles.

'Come in, Michael,' he said, pushing away the lens with the back of his hand. He put down the scalpel and swab, and covered the area of the body he was working on with a white waterproof cloth.

'Come round to the other side of the table,' he said. 'And I'll show you what I mean.'

Angel crossed the wet tiles carefully and took up the position.

Mac turned back the cover to show the head and shoulders of a body. The neck was on a white block shaped to keep it in position facing upwards.

'This is the first victim, Gladys Grant,' he said. Then with tight, rubber-gloved hands, he held tight her nose with one hand and with the other, pulled down her jaw.

'Look there now,' Mac said.

Rice grains seemed to move upwards and spill out of her mouth, which was filled to capacity.

Angel wrinkled his nose involuntarily. 'I see what you mean.'

Mac closed the mouth, then crossed to the other operating table where there was another body.

'Come round here, Michael,' Mac said.

Angel followed him across the room. Mac uncovered the head and shoulders of the other body.

'Now, this is the second victim, Fay Hough,' Mac said. He repeated the demonstration.

Grains of rice spilled out of her mouth.

Angel stared at the figure. He pursed his lips. 'And the rice had nothing to do with the death of either of the victims?' he said.

'Nothing,' Mac said.

Angel rubbed an eyebrow and said, 'I don't understand it.'

The doctor closed the dead woman's mouth and turned the sheet back over the victim's head and shoulders.

The operating theatre not being conducive for discussions, Mac said, 'Let's go into the office.'

Angel followed Mac to the glass windowed office in the corner of the operating theatre.

When the door was closed, the sound of the machinery and water being sloshed around was excluded but the smell was still with them.

Mac took up his seat at a desk. 'Sit down, Michael,' he said. 'I'll get you that note.'

The doctor was still wearing his rubber gloves. He took the keys out of the middle drawer of the desk, selected one, stood up, turned round and unlocked a safe that was behind his chair. Then he reached inside and produced a small, white plastic box. He put it at the end of the desk in front of Angel.

'I have gloves and two pairs of tweezers for you,' Mac said.

Angel slipped on the rubber gloves, opened the box, and with the tweezers took out the folded paper and opened it up.

Like the other note, it was neatly printed by hand in black on plain white paper. He read it out loud. It said:

Gladys Grant, it had to be said,
Was a vicious bitch and had to be dead.
She is the first, and there are five more to go.

Angel's muscles tightened. He ran a hand through his hair. '*Five* more to go, Mac, it says. *Five more to go*!'

'The other note said *four* more to go.'

'The notes have been found out of sequence. The point is the murderer has *six* people in her sights in total.'

'That's only what she has declared in her notes.'

Angel sighed. 'I can't live with that. I have got to anticipate where she will strike next. There must have been some place, situation, gathering, circumstance where she has been with the six women, maybe more than six, but minimally these six women and herself. A place where she — in her madness — was hurt, offended, stolen from, ridiculed, whatever . . . had reason to hate these six enough to want them dead.'

'She didn't have to *know* them, Michael,' Mac said. 'They could be on a list in front of her to get a council house or something like that.'

Angel acknowledged Mac's possibly important contribution with a nod.

'I've got to look at the lives of Gladys Grant and Fay Hough and see what is similar,' Angel said. 'And I've got to do that *before* another woman is murdered.'

It was after six o'clock when Angel left the mortuary.

He drove straight home a worried man.

Mary liked to serve up their tea at around 5.30. It sometimes meant a spoiled meal if he was late. He made an apology for being late and pulled up to the table in the kitchen. Mary wasn't pleased and as she served out the meal, she slapped the mashed potatoes on the plate, banged the spoon on the plate, and rattled the pots and pans around generally in retaliation, but he didn't choose to notice.

When they were settled with their coffee in the sitting room, and a news reader was looking at them from their television set, Angel said, 'Any post?'

Mary got up and brought him an envelope from the sideboard. It was a window envelope and he recognized the sender.

He pulled a face. 'It's from the gas company,' he said.

He put it down. He wasn't in any hurry to open it, although he knew he would have to. He put it down on the table at his side.

'And I've got a message for you,' Mary said.

Angel frowned. 'Yes?'

'It's from that friend of yours, with the little antique shop in town.'

That was Daniel Ashton. Angel's eyes shot up and then came down again. He hoped that Daniel had been discreet and not mentioned anything about diamond rings.

'Oh yes?' Angel said, trying to sound nonchalant.

'He said he's got some information for you. His home number's on the pad.'

'Thanks, love,' he said. 'It'll wait until tomorrow.'

Mary frowned. 'That's unusual for you. You always phone back people you like straightaway.'

Angel returned to the letter from the gas company. He began to open it. He hoped it would divert Mary's interest from the phone call.

'Let's see what they have to say for themselves,' he said. 'Oh, hell. It's the monthly bill,' he said as he began to unfold the contents. 'We've just paid them more than my annual pay as a sergeant for a new boiler because we had to. It was supposed to save us more than thirty-six per cent. Let's see how much this is . . . if it is that much less . . . Oh no. Oh, Mary!'

She looked up from her coffee.

'It's gone *up*. It's not less. It's *more*! The damned thing is *more*! How is it a company like that can get away with making claims like that, that are blatantly untrue?'

'I expect the basic cost of gas has gone up,' Mary said. 'That bill is probably thirty-six per cent less than it would have been if we still had the old boiler.'

Angel stared at her open-mouthed. 'Whose side are you are on?' he said.

'I'm on the side of sweet reasonableness, I hope,' she said.

Angel's fists tightened. 'Sounds as if you are one of the overpaid majority that work for the gas company.'

'Not at all. To be scrupulously fair you have to take all factors into consideration. Also, I think it was much warmer last April than this April, which means our consumption is much higher.'

'I haven't told you,' he said, 'but I've turned the thermostat *down* two degrees, to save us a few pounds.'

'And I haven't told you that I knew,' she said, 'and I turned the thermostat *up* two degrees to prevent us dying from pneumonia!'

‘Huh. You’re the only person I have ever known who turns up the central heating and then wants the windows open! I am not paying out good money to heat up next door’s garden.’

‘Don’t be ridiculous, Michael. You’ve got to have fresh air.’

‘If you want fresh air, you should put on your overcoat and go for a brisk walk.’

Mary’s eyes flashed. ‘Oh!’ she said. She gulped the last drop of coffee, banged the cup on to the saucer, stood up and rushed out into the kitchen.

Angel looked up at her, frowned and watched her leave. Moments later, he heard the running of water, followed by a banging of pots and pans and a loud slamming of kitchen cupboard doors.

He licked his bottom lip thoughtfully, rubbed his chin, stood up, picked up his empty coffee cup and saucer and went into the kitchen.

Mary glared at him, snatched the cup and saucer out of his hands and plunged them into the water in the sink.

Angel walked away from her thoughtfully. He went into the sitting room for a few seconds then he came out, back up to the sink, and said, ‘Would you like me to dry for you, love?’

It was seven o’clock, the same day, and Cliff Grant was in the little dining kitchen at the back of the shop, stretched out on the settee, his head on one arm and his feet overhanging the other. He had a pack of six cans of Monty’s lager on his stomach and was steadily progressing through them, while impatiently pressing buttons on the TV remote. He was desperately trying to get away from the yakety-yak of clean-shaven men in suits, and women with straight dark hair who were talking politics and nothing but politics ahead of the general election the next day.

At Cliff Grant's side, the kitchen table was covered with dirty plates, dirty cutlery and dirty pans as well as opened packets, boxes, tins and jars of all kinds of foodstuffs.

The shop bell rang. He looked at the clock. It said twenty past seven. He tossed the remote onto the table, dragged the part pack of lager off his stomach and allowed it to drop onto the floor. Then he pushed himself off the settee and ambled into the shop.

Looking at him across the counter were the twinkling and tantalizing eyes of Maisie Spencer, the one of the low-cut blouse and short skirt tradition. The one who claimed that they had been engaged. She was smiling.

Cliff Grant looked her up and down and grinned.

Neither seemed to be in a hurry to speak first.

'Hello,' Grant said.

Maisie said, 'Hello.'

Grant said, 'Well, well, well, what brings you out of the house at this time of night?'

Maisie Spencer came up close to the counter and still smiling, said, 'Would you believe I have been cooking beef stew . . . it's been in the oven for almost three hours and I thought of you.'

'Now why would you think of me?' Grant said.

'Oh, I thought of you . . . all on your own, stuck here, doing your own cooking . . . and there's far too much beef stew for one.'

'That's nice of you to think of me.'

More smiles. More silence. He looked at her ample bosom, and grinned all the more. She looked at his strong tanned face, fabulous physique, thick shiny hair, big grin and faultless teeth.

'There was another reason I thought of you,' Maisie said, then she giggled.

Grant looked at her more closely, and she giggled even more. She couldn't stop herself. The giggling became worse. She put a hand over her mouth. He laughed with her but he didn't know the reason for it.

'What's so funny?' he said. 'What was the *other* reason you thought of me?'

Amidst more giggling, she said, 'It was because I wanted—'

She broke off again with the giggles.

Grant lifted up the hinged piece of counter, opened the little door and came through to the customer side. He put both of her hands round his neck, put his own hands round her shoulders and gave her a powerful, lingering kiss on the lips.

When they eased back from the kiss, the giggling had stopped. She looked both stunned and stunning. She was breathing quickly. Her bosom was rising and falling. She stared into his soft blue eyes.

Grant's pulse was racing. 'Oh, Maisie,' he said. 'Oh, Maisie . . . can you . . . can you stay a while?'

'Oh yes,' she said. 'A couple of hours. Must get back for ten. Mum phones me at ten. She'd be worried if she didn't get a reply.'

He tightened his hold around her, squeezing her breasts against his chest. She ran her hands up and down his thick, brown muscular arms.

He slackened the hold and began to undo the buttons of her blouse.

'Not here, Cliff,' she said, gently taking his hands in hers.

He agreed. He looked at her and said, 'Upstairs?'

She nodded.

Then he pointed to the gap in the counter and said, 'Go on through, Maisie,' he said. 'Straight through the sitting room and up the stairs. You'll see. I'll be right behind you. It's quarter to eight. What's fifteen minutes? I'll lock up. Turn out the lights.'

Maisie squeezed through the break in the counter.

Grant quickly turned the sign in the glass door round to show CLOSED outside, turned the key in the lock and withdrew it, shot the bolts across at the top and the bottom, dashed through the break in the counter and switched off the lights.

SIX

It was 8.28, Thursday morning, 7 May.

Angel was already in his office at Bromersley Police Station. He was preparing the lines of action he intended to pursue and he had just phoned DC Ahmed Ahaz in CID to come into his office.

There was a knock on the door and the young man appeared. He was carrying his notebook.

'Yes, sir,' he said.

'Ah yes, Ahmed,' Angel said. 'I want to see Don Taylor as soon as he gets here. That'll take about ten minutes. Then at about 8.40, I want to see Flora Carter, Trevor Crisp and Ted Scrivens. Put the word out.'

'Right, sir,' Ahmed said.

'And then I want you to phone Mixendon's Glass Works on Wells Road. Speak to the CEO and find out where their employee Lance Hough is and how he can be contacted urgently. Don't tell them anything about the reason we need to know. Just say it is very important and that it is police business, all right?'

'Got it, sir.'

'Then I want you to see if you can trace a Philip Grant. He lived at 83 Sebastopol Terrace, Bromersley. Ran a small grocer's business from there. Now around thirty years ago, he divorced or deserted his wife, Gladys Grant. Her maiden name was Hemingway. I am told that he died ten or fifteen years ago in Leeds, aged around fifty or sixty. It's not much to go on, but see what you can do. I should start at Bromersley's Births, Deaths and Marriages. I assume he married Gladys around 1984. Have you got all that?'

'Yes, sir. Anything else?'

'No, lad. That'll do for starters.'

Ahmed grinned and dashed off.

A few moments later, there was a knock at the door. It was DS Taylor.

'Come in, Don,' Angel said. 'Sit down. A couple of things. First of all, that rice?'

'It's regular rice, sir, sold in packets in grocery outlets usually, and imported by the shipload mostly from Thailand, but also from Burma and China. There would be no chance of tracing it.'

Angel nodded and pulled a sour face. At every turn, he felt thwarted. It would have been difficult for him to pretend that he was not disappointed.

'What about the graphologist? Have you heard from him yet?'

'Just come in, sir. He knew it was urgent so he phoned me a few minutes ago. I made some notes.' He took out a little notebook and referred to it. 'He said that it was extremely difficult for him to work without several samples. A formal letter would have been ideal—'

Angel eyes flashed. The muscles in his face tightened. 'We haven't got a formal letter. If we'd had a formal letter, we would have known the killer's name and we wouldn't have a need to waste time bothering him, would we?'

Taylor waited.

Angel wiped a hand across his mouth and chin. 'Did he say anything positive?'

'He said it was definitely a man—'

Angel's eyes flashed again. 'A *man*?' he said. 'But the witnesses have told us they saw a *woman*!'

Taylor lifted his eyebrows and his shoulders a little and turned the palms of his hands upwards.

Angel breathed out noisily then said, 'Anything else?'

'And that he would be of a mature age. Also that there are certain distinctive aspects of the upper loops of the lower-case letters f, h, k and l that puzzle him and make him wonder if the writer is not emotionally unstable.'

'Ah,' Angel said. 'So we agree on *one* thing, then. Our murderer is emotionally unstable. Surprise, surprise!'

'And that's it, sir,' Taylor said closing the notebook.

Angel sniffed. 'Graphology is supposed to be a respected profession.'

Taylor said, 'It was very helpful in that Aspinall case, sir. The info given was correct in every particular, if you remember.'

Taylor was quite correct, Angel remembered.

There was a knock at the door and it was DS Carter; she was closely followed by DS Crisp and DC Scrivens.

'Come in. Come in,' Angel said, then he turned back to Taylor and said, 'Are we done, Don?'

'Yes, sir,' he said. 'I'll push off, if that's all right.'

Taylor went out and closed the door.

Angel looked round. 'Will you sit down, Flora?' He turned to the two men standing. 'Sorry, there are only two chairs. You two lads will have to fight over who sits down and who stands.'

DC Scrivens said, 'It's all right, sir, I'll stand.'

When they were all settled, Angel turned to Flora and said, 'Did you finish the door to door?'

'Yes, sir,' she said. 'There are only six apartments on that floor. We called on the other five. And nobody saw or heard anything. Everybody there seemingly keep themselves to themselves so we couldn't find out anything about the Houghs.'

Crisp said, 'Nobody I called on saw or heard anything. Of course it *was* early in the morning. They're mostly elderly people in those flats. They don't get out of bed until about eight o'clock.'

Angel wrinkled his nose. 'What about newspaper deliveries?'

Flora and Trevor Crisp glanced at each other.

Crisp said, 'Newsagents don't deliver newspapers these days, sir.'

'I am sure some do,' Angel said. 'Depends on where you live. Anyway, did either of you check on it?'

They both shook their heads.

Angel wasn't pleased. He shook his head in surprise then looked at Scrivens. 'Right, Ted. Head off and see which newsagents deliver newspapers to that building, then interview all the kids that made any delivery early yesterday morning. And find out who they saw in the building, or entering or leaving the building at the critical time. And get a full description. Do it quickly, while it's fresh in their minds. Off you go.'

Scrivens nodded. 'Right, sir,' he said and he went out.

Angel then looked at his two sergeants and said, 'Right. We have to move fast. We have two murders on our hands. Both committed by the same woman in the same way. And you have both seen the notes or copies of the notes left by her. They clearly indicate that she intends to murder six people. Now the murderer must have a motive, grudge or whatever against those six women. She must have had — or still has — some sort of a relationship with them. So, maybe the seven were in the same bus, house, home, family, institution, hospital, school, work, doctor's waiting room, train, plane, ship, hotel, whatever when something happened. Maybe if we can find out *what* it was, or *where* it was, we can prevent the rest of the women on her list being killed. So we need to find the common denominator between the two victims, which should of course, apply to the other four intended victims *and* possibly, the murderer as well.'

Angel stopped. His face shone with enthusiasm. He was optimistic about his plan to discover the identity of the murderer. And he hoped that they would be. He looked at them and rubbed his chin. 'Are you with me so far?'

'Yes, sir,' Flora said.

Crisp said, 'But sir, there doesn't on the face of it seem to be much similarity between the lifestyles of Gladys Grant and Fay Hough. Mrs Grant was a widow bringing up a child, and working as a self-employed shopkeeper living in what would now be regarded as sub-standard housing. Mrs Hough was the wife of an executive in a big company and living in a luxury apartment. It's difficult to imagine where their paths crossed.'

'I didn't say it would be easy, Trevor,' Angel said. He turned away from Crisp and looked at Carter. He wanted to know what she thought about the plan.

Angel's phone rang. He glared at it. It always rang at a critical moment. He reached out for it. 'Angel,' he said.

It was Superintendent Harker. Angel knew it was him from the breathy sound he frequently made when inhaling.

'Ah, yes, Angel,' Harker said. 'There's been a triple nine from a man at 62 Cemetery Road.'

Angel's heart sunk to his boots.

Harker said, 'Name of Lunn, Dale Lunn. He says he's found his wife, Felicity, covered with blood, on her bed, a few minutes ago. Ambulance on its way. Call timed at 08.40 hours. Get on with it.'

He terminated the call.

Angel slowly replaced the phone. He turned to face the sergeants. Flora Carter and Trevor Crisp stared back at him. The blood drained from his face until his cheeks were the colour of chip shop lard.

Angel soon recovered and triggered the mechanism to begin the investigation into the death of Felicity Lunn.

Sergeants Flora Carter and Trevor Crisp had been immediately directed onto door-to-door inquiries along Cemetery Road.

By the time Angel arrived in the BMW on Cemetery Road, he discovered that all hell had broken loose outside number 62.

Every possible parking space within a five-minute walk had a vehicle of some sort parked in it. Many had a local or national PRESS card displayed on the windscreen. Some had a TV news company's logo. Some must have been local residents. There were six marked police vehicles not far from the scene of the crime, also several other unmarked cars on police business, including those of Dr Mac and the CID cars. Angel also saw a white van with a large dish aerial extended on its roof and he wondered what it was that might be in the process of being recorded or transmitted.

Although Angel had a police pass and could theoretically park where he needed to while on duty, he found it impossible to find a place close to number 62 that wouldn't also cause a potential traffic hazard.

He drove slowly round the block for a third time and was then elated when he saw a man walk up to a car quite close to number 62. The man unlocked the car door and climbed into the driving seat. Angel edged the BMW nearer. The man didn't seem to do anything for a half minute, then he saw him reach up for his seat belt. Angel sighed and edged even further towards him. Seconds later the car's amber indicators began to flash. Angel saw a wheel move. Then the car pulled out and the man drove away. Promptly he motored into the space. He parked up, put the POLICE ON DUTY sign on the windscreen and climbed out of the car.

As he approached the house, he could see that round the front gate was a congested mob of people. Some were holding up their mobile phones. Pressmen and women and photographers (some standing on portable sets of aluminium steps) were pointing their cameras at the house. He also saw several reporters with microphones and at least two handheld television videotape cameras in position on the overflowing pavement.

There was one lone uniformed policeman standing on the front door step which was about two metres from the gate. He was trying not to notice the mob in front of him. He reacted quickly enough, however, when Angel put a hand on the gate to open it.

'You can't—' the police officer said. He broke off. 'Oh. Sorry, sir. Didn't realize it was you.' He saluted.

Angel heard voices behind him. 'Who is this? He's a detective. It's Inspector Angel. Get him. It's Angel. Hey, Inspector Angel! Inspector Angel!'

He turned to face them.

Cameras began to click. It seemed everybody held up a mobile phone.

'What can you tell us about this murder, Inspector?' somebody said.

Microphones of all types, size and colour were thrust under his nose.

'I don't know if it is a murder yet,' Angel said. 'I have only just arrived. It hasn't been determined.'

'What about the other two women?' another voice said.

'Were they murdered by the same man?'

Angel held up a hand. 'You mustn't interfere with us trying to do our job. You cannot hold this house under siege like this. I understand your interest, but you are making it difficult here. You are also interfering with the residents' privacy and peace and quiet on this street. I can tell you that no interviews or answers to your questions will be given from this house. Anybody who does not leave this site within the next five minutes will be arrested and charged with hindering the police in the execution of their business and/or being a public nuisance.'

There was uproar from them. 'That's not fair. We're speaking for the people, we've a right to know. It's not safe to sleep in our beds at night.'

Angel held up a hand to speak. Out came the microphones again.

'What I will do is hold a press conference this afternoon at the police station at 1600 hours, when I will be as forthcoming as I can. Now please pack up and leave here *now*. Thank you.'

Then he turned round, patted the back of the PC on duty there, put his hand on the door handle, pushed open the door and went into the little terraced house.

On hearing the door of 62 Cemetery Road open and close, one of the SOCO team members came through from the back. 'Oh. Good morning, sir. DS Taylor and Dr Mac are upstairs where the victim is situated.'

'Thank you. Have you finished the vacuuming and print taking?'

'Yes, sir. You won't need gloves.'

Angel nodded and made for the stairs. When he had reached the top, he said, 'Is it all done? Can I come in?'

'Of course, sir,' Taylor said.

Taylor and Mac looked at the inspector as he opened the bedroom door.

'And I am ready for off, Michael,' Mac said.

They moved back from the bed in the little room to let Angel see the victim.

The body was that of a skinny woman in a nightdress, sitting upright. It was in the bed, propped against the bed head with pillows. There was blood all over the nightdress and a cauliflower in her lap.

Angel went close up to her and looked in every direction. Then he leaned back, pursed his lips, and looked at the doctor.

'All right, Mac,' he said. 'What have you got?'

Mac said, 'Married woman, aged sixty, stabbed three times in the heart. Exactly the same as the other two. Been dead approximately six or seven hours. That means she was murdered between five and eight o'clock this morning.'

Angel nodded then said, 'I see the cauliflower. What about the rice?'

Mac said, 'Oh yes. A gullet and a mouth full of rice.'

He turned up his nose and shook his head. He looked at Taylor. 'Was access the same as Fay Hough?'

'Yes, sir. A crowbar round the lock on the back door.'

He rubbed his chin. 'And is there a note?'

Taylor said, 'I've got that, sir.'

Mac said, 'Can I have the body?'

Angel wiped his chin with his hand. 'I don't see why not, Mac,' he said. 'Yes, of course. Soon as you like.'

Mac nodded, took out his mobile and went out of the room onto the landing.

Angel turned back to Taylor. 'I want to see that note.'

'It was tucked down the neck of the nightdress,' Taylor said. 'We opened it, and I copied it out. If it's all right with you, we'll x-ray this paper and see if that tells us anything new.'

'Good idea, Don, but let me read what it says.'

He passed Angel his notebook, holding it open at the page where it was copied.

'There, sir,' Taylor said.

Angel looked at it and then read it out aloud:

Felicity Lunn was too much fun,

Nasty, dirty, and had to be done.

Felicity is third, and there are three more to go.

He read it again silently then handed it back. He was thinking . . . the note said, three more to go. He gritted his teeth at the thought of it.

He looked round the tiny room. He had to squeeze between the double bed, the bedside cupboard, the dressing-table and the wardrobe. As he passed the window, he looked out at the view of the cemetery and at the street below. There were still cars and people hanging around. He wasn't pleased.

Angel stuck out his chin and the muscles of his jaw and neck tightened. He thrust his hand into his pocket and took out his mobile.

'Just look at them, Don. Like ghouls,' he said. 'There's a bit of a throng outside. I've tried to thin it out.'

He went out of the room and ambled across the landing into a tiny single-bedded room, the only other room upstairs besides the bathroom. He left the door open and sat on the bed.

He opened the phone and scrolled down to Inspector Asquith at the station. He was in charge of the uniformed branch of the force at Bromersley.

'Hello, Michael, what's up?' Asquith said.

'Haydn, the young constable you have on the door of 62 Cemetery Road needs some assistance, also there is a build-up of the media outside the place and the pathologist wants to collect the body soon. Could you send some lads round and sort it out?'

Asquith said, 'You couldn't have called at a worse time, Michael. I'm six men down away on a course, three off sick and those Sheffield Road traffic lights are not working.'

'Well, do what you can, Haydn, please.'

'I'll sort it. Cheers.'

Angel closed his phone. He ruminated quietly, rubbing his chin for a few moments, then he stood up, and went back into the bedroom where the murder had been committed. Taylor was standing, looking down at the clipboard he was holding.

Angel said, 'Well, Don, have you anything else unusual to tell me?'

Taylor looked round. 'No, sir. Nothing pertaining to the attacker has been vacuumed from the body.'

Angel glared at him. 'Nothing?' he said.

Taylor stopped the searching and turned round to look at Angel. 'Nothing that we can be certain came from her attacker.'

Angel wrinkled his nose. 'You are methodically searching the bins, Don, aren't you? And checking for prints on anything that could have been left by the killer?'

'Yes, sir,' Taylor said. 'In this instance, we have emptied the rubbish into a large evidence bag and we are taking it back to the station where we can examine it item by item more easily.'

Angel nodded then put a hand to his forehead and rubbed it with his fingers. 'Where was the husband when all this was happening?' he said.

'He has a perfect alibi, sir,' Taylor said. 'He's a bus driver and he was on a scheduled service, taking forty-four passengers on an early shift to work at that massive warehouse they've built at Little Copton.'

'Oh,' he said, pushing out his lower lip. 'Where is he now?'

'With his married daughter, at her house.'

Angel's mobile rang out.

'Excuse me,' he said, then he turned back to the open door, went back into the little bedroom and sat on the bed. He took the phone out of his pocket, opened it. He saw who was calling him. He pressed the button and said, 'What is it, Ahmed?'

'If it's not convenient, sir—' Ahmed said.

'No, it's fine, lad. What is it?'

'You wanted to know about Gladys Grant's husband, Philip Grant, who had lived at 83 Sebastopol Terrace, sir.'

'Yes. What have you got?'

'He left Bromersley in 1986, sir, Gladys divorced him in 1987. I lost him for a while, but then he popped up applying for a licence to sell wines and spirits at a corner shop in Leeds in 1988. Lived there until he died in 2005 aged fifty-four.'

'He's definitely dead?'

'I've got a copy of his death certificate, sir. Under cause of death, it says, atheroma, myocarditis and broncho-pneumonia. Dates and addresses all fit.'

Angel sighed. Another dead end, he was thinking. 'Right, Ahmed. Thank you,' he said. 'Good work.'

'And you wanted to know about Lance Hough, sir. Well, I phoned Mixendon's and they said that he *was* in Paris, staying at the Hotel La Fayette, and calling on a customer close by. But he has left there and they don't quite know where he is. They think he must be on his way back home.'

Angel rubbed his forehead gently with his fingers. 'All right, Ahmed. Thank you. Now, there's something else. I've told the media that there'll be a press conference this afternoon at four o'clock. Will you make sure the parade room will be available? We'll need about forty chairs and a table at the front. You've seen how we do it, haven't you?'

'Oh *yes*, sir,' Ahmed said. 'Will do.'

'Right,' he said, 'I'll leave it with you.'

He ended the call, closed the phone and put it back in his pocket. It rang out immediately. He pulled it out again, saw that it was Scrivens calling. He pressed the button and said, 'Yes, Ted?'

'I have found a witness, sir, he's the actual newsagent. He does the early morning deliveries to Monserrat Flats himself. He says boys are no longer reliable.'

Angel blinked. Possibly good news, he thought. 'Great. What did he see?'

'He said a queer-looking woman in a long sheepskin coat passed him, rushing down the steps leaving, as he went into the building,' Scrivens said.

Angel's eyes narrowed. 'Did he comment on the woman's hair or anything else about her?'

'No, sir. I pressed him as much as I could.'

'Why did he describe her as "queer-looking"?'

'I'm not sure, sir.'

'I'd better see him. What's his name and where is he?'

'Alec Moore, sir, and his shop address is 77/79 Sheffield Road.'

SEVEN

Angel stopped the BMW outside Moore's Newsagents on Sheffield Road. He locked the car and went into the shop.

Alec Moore was straightening the newspapers on the counter.

Angel introduced himself and said, 'Thank you for assisting us, Mr Moore. What I would like to know is if you saw the woman's face.'

'No, Inspector,' he said. 'She never turned to look at me. She was in too much of a hurry to get away from the building.'

'What colour was her hair?'

Moore frowned. 'I'm not sure. Grey, I think. She was certainly no chicken, but she could move fast when she wanted to.'

'Was she a big woman?'

'Well, yes. She certainly wasn't skinny. Yes. I suppose you'd say she was well-made.'

'I understand that you told my sergeant that she was "queer-looking". What did you mean by that? You told me that you didn't see her face.'

Moore ran a hand over his face. 'Ah, yes,' he said. 'It's hard to explain, Inspector. I didn't see her face. I suppose what I meant was that there was something incongruous about her age, her size and the speed she was able to make down those steps.'

Angel frowned. He didn't think he was going to get any additional information from him so he thanked him, came out of the shop and returned to the police station.

He drove the BMW onto his allocated parking space at the back of the station and made his way through the back door, past the cells and down the corridor.

Ahmed saw him through the open door of the CID room and ran out into the corridor.

'Excuse me, sir,' Ahmed said. 'There's a Mr Lance Hough in reception waiting to see you.'

Angel stopped. 'Lance Hough?' he said, then he pursed his lips. He wanted to see him. He looked at his watch. It was twenty past three. 'Is everything ready for the press conference, Ahmed?'

'Yes, sir. Would you like to have a look?'

'I had hoped to use the next half hour or so to prepare what I wanted to say,' Angel said.

'Mr Hough has been waiting about half an hour, sir.'

'You'd better bring him down, Ahmed. You'll have to make it quick.'

'Right, sir,' Ahmed said and he dashed off.

Angel went into his office. He picked up the phone and dialled a single digit. It was soon answered. 'SOCO, DS Taylor.'

'Ah, you're back, Don,' he said. 'I will shortly have Lance Hough in my office. You want his prints for elimination purposes, don't you?'

'Oh *yes*, sir,' Taylor said.

'I'll send him up to your office in the next twenty minutes or so.' Angel returned the phone to its holster and quickly piled the papers on his desk into one heap which he then slid across to the far corner.

There was a knock on his door. It was Ahmed with a smartly dressed, sun-tanned man in his sixties.

'Mr Hough, sir,' Ahmed said.

'Thank you, Ahmed,' Angel said, then he turned to the man and said, 'Come in, Mr Hough. Please sit down.'

The man chose the chair nearest the desk and sat down.

Ahmed went out and closed the door.

Angel said, 'Let me say how sorry I am, Mr Hough. And assure you that my team and I are doing our best to find your wife's murderer.'

'Thank you. I regret being away from home. If I had been here this would never have happened. I have presented myself here to you as soon as I could get here, to see if there is anything I could do to assist in your inquiries.'

'Thank you very much for that. Not many next of kin are as helpful as that. How did you find out about your wife's passing?'

'I phoned Fay this morning about eight o'clock, your time. There's was no reply. I tried several times but there was still no reply. I was worried, so eventually I rang our friend, Delia Ivory. She told me what had happened. Naturally, I dropped everything there and made a bee line for home. I saw Delia. She told me that you were dealing with it. I was pleased about that. I've heard of your reputation. Now what can I do to help?'

'Well, firstly, we'll need your fingerprints for elimination purposes.'

Hough leaned back in the chair and put a hand to his chin. His forehead creased as he said, 'Oh, is that absolutely necessary?'

Angel said, 'It's only used to determine prints left by you. After all, you live there and your prints are bound to be all over the place. Of course, when the case is over, all the elimination prints taken are torn up and burned.'

'Are they really?'

'Oh yes,' Angel said. 'Now, I heard you say that you've been back to your flat, Mr Hough. Did you have a good look round? Did you find that anything had been taken?'

'I didn't notice anything missing. My silver golf trophies were all there. We don't have any cash, or silver or gold or works of art or anything of that sort, Inspector.'

'Did you find anything that had been *left* by the killer?'

'No.'

'Can you think of any reason why anyone would want to murder your wife?'

'No. I can't. Certainly not.'

'And where exactly where you at 5.30 this morning?'

'I was in bed asleep in room 414 in the Hotel La Fayette, in Paris.'

'Do you have a witness who can corroborate the fact?'

Hough blinked. He thought a moment and said, 'I wasn't sharing my bed with anyone, Inspector.'

'I didn't for one moment think that you were, Mr Hough. But you may have had room service attend to you during the night, or a porter may have given you an early morning call.'

Hough shook his head. 'No, I didn't see anyone during the night.'

Angel rubbed his chin. 'Pity,' he said.

Hough's lips curled with anger. He clenched his fists. 'I had dinner in the hotel last night,' he said, 'so I was in the restaurant until about 9.30, and breakfast there at 7.30 this morning. The staff would confirm that, I'm sure. I hope you don't think that during the night, I got a taxi to Charles de Gaulle airport, then a plane to Leeds/Bradford, and a taxi to Bromersley, killed my own darling wife, then taxied back to Leeds/Bradford airport, flew to Paris and took another taxi back to the hotel. Taking the requirement to pass through security, passports and customs four times, I'm not even sure that there would have been sufficient time.'

'Of course I don't, Mr Hough. But I have to check. And what were you actually doing that required you to be there?'

'It was to do with my work. I was sewing up a deal with the fashion house Le Bon on behalf of Mixendon's Glass Works. We are to supply them with uniquely shaped and tinted bottles for their top of the range perfumes.'

'Right, Mr Hough. I think that's about it for now,' he said, reaching out for the phone. He tapped in Ahmed's number.

'Will you take Mr Hough up to SOCO? Don Taylor is expecting him.'

'Right, sir.'

Angel replaced the phone. He looked at Hough and said, 'Thank you for coming in.'

They stood up.

'Detective Constable Ahaz is on his way. He will show you where you need to be.'

'Thank you, Inspector. I hope you find the bastard who murdered my wife.'

In his heart of hearts, Angel thought, 'So do I,' but he actually found himself saying, 'We will, sir. We will.'

They shook hands.

It was 3.55 p.m. and the parade room at Bromersley Police Station was buzzing with reporters, photographers, and men with videotape cameras on their shoulders. There was an air of excitement and lots of loud chatter among the people in the business of news gathering.

Ahmed was standing by the open door.

At exactly 4 p.m. Angel arrived. He stopped at the door and glanced at the crowd. He was pleased with the turnout.

He looked at Ahmed and said, 'Everything all right, lad?'

'I think so, sir,' Ahmed said. 'Is there anything you want? Have I forgotten anything?'

'Everything looks fine. When you're ready, close the door.'

Angel crossed to the table, looked round the room and nodded to several familiar faces. He saw the jug of water and upturned glass tumbler on a sheet of kitchen roll, the dozen or so microphones, and the innumerable recording devices that had been placed in front of him on the table. They made him mindful of what he must *not* say. He ran a hand over his mouth and chin, then sat down behind the table.

Ahmed went out into the corridor to see if there were any latecomers. There weren't any, so he went back into the room and closed the door.

The chattering died down to silence, then Angel stood up and said, 'Ladies and gentlemen, I want to thank you all for coming.'

Then he told the journalists the facts of the three murder cases in detail and highlighted their several similarities, including the fact that all three murders had been executed between 5 and 8 a.m. He also pointed out that the murders were always executed when the victim was alone. However, he studiously avoided mentioning the sighting of a grey-haired woman in a long sheepskin coat seen leaving two of the three crime scenes shortly after the time of death.

The audience was attentive and quiet. He then said that he was expecting a further three murders if he could not quickly discover the identity of the killer.

He put his hands flat on the table top, leaned forward and said, 'I want to make an appeal, and I want you to spread it quickly and prominently, if you will. It is to all middle-aged women. If you are a woman of about sixty years of age, and knew the three women who have been murdered, you could be next on the murderer's list. Please dial 999 and ask for the police. The police can protect you and they will, but you must come forward and make yourself known to them.'

He then thanked them for their kind attention and sat down. He poured some water into the tumbler and took a good drink.

There was a subdued rumble of whisperings from the gathering.

Then Angel said, 'I would be happy to answer any questions you may have.'

They were mostly questions about the method used by the killer to commit the murders, the cauliflower, the rice and the victims' histories and lifestyles. They presented no difficulty to him. When he noticed that the questions were becoming hypothetical or he thought that he had already adequately answered them, he courteously brought the question-and-answer session to an end.

The pressmen and women couldn't get out with their trappings to file their stories quickly enough, and the parade room was emptied in quick time.

It was eight o'clock on that same warm, sunny evening of Thursday 7 May. As the poet Alfred Lord Tennyson wrote, 'In the Spring, a young man's fancy lightly turns to thoughts of love.' And so it was that Cliff Grant's head had been turned that long May day by the sight across the shop counter of girls and young women who had been in the shop. The discarding of their coats and warm clothing had showed far too much sensuous skin and shapely limbs and bodies than they had realized, which had stirred the masculine inclinations in his head, his heart and his body. Such that that particular Thursday evening Cliff Grant had a powerful personal need of womanly comfort and attention, so at eight o'clock promptly, he locked the shop, had a quick shower, a shave, put on his best suit and taking an expensive box of chocolates out of the shop stock, he set off along Canal Street.

He knew exactly where he was going. It was to number 120. The home of the highly desirable Ann Fiske. He took a deep breath as he lifted the knocker on her door and gave it a hard one-two-three.

He stood there, listening for some sound that signified she was in. There was no certainty that she was. He reckoned it was possible that some virile school teacher or even a parent of one of her pupils had taken a serious interest in her and whisked her away.

Suddenly he heard a bolt being drawn, the click of a key in a lock and then the door opened three inches on a chain. A pair of beautiful, bright brown eyes peered through the crack at him.

Grant smiled. 'It's me, Tutshy Face,' he said.

'Oh, Cliff,' Ann Fiske said. 'Just a minute.'

He thought she seemed pleased to see him. That was a good start.

The door was pushed to release the safety chain, then opened wide to reveal her in a light, floral patterned dress that curved sensuously around her thighs.

His pulse increased at the sight of her.

Ann Fiske looked him up and down and enjoyed his straight back, muscular legs, strong arms, black hair, warm tanned skin and curling smile.

'What's wrong, Cliff?'

Grant smiled. 'Nothing now I've seen you.'

She shook her head and smiled. 'Come in.'

'Thank you,' he said.

She closed the door and dropped the latch. 'Come in here and sit down,' she said and led him into the sitting room.

When he was comfortable she said, 'I'm terribly sorry to hear about your mother. It's absolutely dreadful. Are you all right?'

'I've come to terms with it, Tutshy Face. We didn't see eye to eye on many things, and she was difficult to live with at times, but the bond between us was strong. It must've been or I wouldn't have come back.'

'What's happening to the shop?'

She noticed the box under his arm.

'I don't know,' Grant said. 'I'm trying to keep it going for the time being.'

'Well, you know where to come if you're stuck anytime.'

'Thank you, Tutshy Face.'

He took the box of chocolates from under his arm and said, 'I've brought you these.'

'You shouldn't have,' Ann said. 'What are they? Oh, my favourites. That is nice of you, Cliff.'

She quickly undid the ribbon, removed the lid and gazed at the mass of decorated and gold foiled chocolates. She offered them to him. 'They look very yummy. After you.'

'Not for me, Ann. Not long since I had tea. Anyway, I brought them for *you*.'

'It's a bit too warm to enjoy chocolates,' she said. 'I'll have one later.'

She replaced the lid on the box and put it on the table. Then turned back, reached up to Grant, put her arms round his neck, pulled him down and kissed him gently on the lips.

'Thank you, Cliff,' she said.

Something welled up in his throat. He pulled her to him. They kissed again. Her body ached for his caresses.

Grant's eyes closed. His arms went round her back. Her body was aflame. She pressed her stomach to his. His heart exploded with a scorching, pleasant lava which spread rapidly through his chest. Her arms tightened and overlapped round his neck. He gently pressed her to his hard body.

In Ann's imagination, she was intoxicated and drifting in and out of consciousness, wearing only a stream of white voile and floating slowly, and rhythmically to paradise. Then she heard the banging of the knocker on her front door.

Her heart leaped. She pulled away from Grant.

'The door,' she said, trying to get her breath.

'I didn't hear anything,' he said, still with his arms round her. His heart beating like a drum.

The banging was repeated, louder.

'Did you hear *that*?' she said as she tried to pull away from him.

'Ignore it,' he said. 'They'll go away.'

'It might be my mother,' she said. 'Let me go, Cliff.' She pulled away from him again. She was worried. 'I *must* answer it.'

Grant released her. He wasn't pleased.

She ran towards the hall. 'Do I look all right?' she said.

'You always look wonderful, Tutshy face,' he said. He breathed in deeply.

He sighed and took out his handkerchief and wiped his forehead.

When she reached the door, she straightened the front of her dress and ran her hands over her hair.

He heard her unlock the door and say, 'Yes?' And he could hear a man's voice reply, but he couldn't make out what was being said.

Grant hoped that whoever it was could be dismissed quickly. He sat down on the settee. He bounced on it a couple of times and nodded with satisfaction. He looked around admiringly at how clean and polished everything was.

He could still hear the mumbling. Then he heard the front door close.

Ann Fiske came back into the sitting room, putting on a raincoat. 'My dad's been taken into hospital again, Cliff. It's his heart. I'll *have* to go to my mother's. I have to try and settle her down. That was their next-door neighbour. He's going to give me a lift in his car. He's waiting for me. Sorry, darling, I really am.'

Grant reckoned it sounded conclusive. 'Oh, I'm sorry too, Tutshy face,' he said. 'Of course, you must do your best for them both.'

'Sorry to push you out,' she said.

He didn't show his disappointment; he opened the front door and went outside.

Ann Fiske followed him with her handbag in one hand and a bunch of keys in the other.

He saw a small car parked against the kerb. The engine was running. There was a bald man with spectacles in the driving seat.

Ann Fiske leaned down and climbed into the car. Grant got hold of the car door handle. She looked up at him and smiled. 'Thank you. See you soon,' she said.

He nodded. 'Call in the shop sometime,' he said and closed the door.

The bald man let in the clutch and the car moved off.

Grant gave her a wave, and remained there until the car took the corner and was out of sight. He looked at his watch. It was eight minutes past eight. The night was young. He knew exactly what he was going to do with the rest of it. He made a determined step towards the far end of Canal Street. He was heading for number 24.

He soon arrived there, and knocked on the door.

It was answered by Maisie Spencer who smiled widely. She couldn't be more pleased to see anybody on that balmy spring evening. She had been thinking of him only minutes ago. 'Come in, Cliff, come in,' she said.

He smiled at her and flashed his best seductive smile. She quickly closed the door and dropped the latch.

'Thank you, Maisie,' he said.

She looked as alluring as always. He immediately felt a stirring in his loins.

'How are you?' he said.

His voice always charmed her. It was warm, clear and seemed to be educated.

'Oh, I'm fine, Cliff. Go on through into the room, and sit down,' she said.

She noticed that his fine-looking black hair had been smartly trimmed, his shoes polished, that he'd had a shave and there was a neat crease in his trousers. She knew he had a powerful physique under that dark navy-blue suit.

'Right,' he said. 'How have you been keeping?'

'Oh, it's been so lonely here on my own, particularly since Angie went to my mother's.'

Angie was reputed to be Maisie's sister, but she was only eight. That would have meant that there was fourteen years between them, and their mother, if she was their mother, was almost fifty-five years of age.

'I hope she's all right,' he said. He cleared some women's magazines and newspapers off the settee and sat down.

'She's fine,' Maisie said. 'What brings you here?'

She plumped a cushion on an easy chair opposite him as she prepared to sit down there. He reached out, took her hand and pulled her down onto the settee by his side.

'It's all right to visit the girl I'm engaged to, once in a while, isn't it?'

Maisie Spencer smiled. She was delighted that he thought of them as being engaged. She knew then that if he made an advance on her that evening, she would not be able to resist him.

‘As we’re engaged, shouldn’t I have a ring to seal it?’ she said.

‘Yep, and as soon as I can, I’m going to get you one,’ he said.

She leaned over and gave him a peck on the cheek. He didn’t let her get away. He put his arms round her and gave her a much longer kiss on the lips. She hung on to him. He stopped, turned her round so that her back was across his lap and her legs stretched out along the length of the settee. They kissed several times, their hearts pumping faster and faster as their passions dictated.

She kicked off her shoes.

Grant applied his warm, gentle hand with dexterity under her skirt along her smooth, long legs.

EIGHT

It was two o'clock in the morning of Friday 8 May.

Moonlight shone brightly through the window onto the bed.

Cliff Grant awoke. He blinked. Momentarily he wondered where he was, and then he remembered everything and smiled. He peered in the dim light at Maisie, beautiful and fast asleep. He smiled.

He gently peeled back the bedclothes and eased himself out of the bed, not wanting to wake her. He walked barefoot over a trail of clothes, some his and some hers to the bathroom. While he was there, he had a good wash. Then in the moonlight he collected the clothes from the floor, putting hers on a chair and retaining his own. He crept quietly downstairs, collecting his suit coat and tie off the stairs on the way. In the sitting room, he checked that the curtains were closed, switched on the light and got dressed. Then he looked round for paper and pen. He found a pen in a tumbler filled with other pencils and crayons on the mantelpiece, and behind a candlestick were several envelopes opened but with contents of some sort. He selected one and in big letters on the back of it he wrote, 'I LOVE YOU,' and he left the envelope leaning across the dial of the sitting room clock. She was bound to see it when she wanted to know the time. He switched off the light and let himself out by the front door. He was in his own bed by 2.30 a.m.

Angel arrived at his office at 8.28 a.m. that Friday morning. Almost as soon as he sat down, his phone went. It was the civilian telephone receptionist.

'Good morning, Inspector,' she said. 'I've a Mr Daniel Ashton on the phone for you. He says he's an old friend. Do you want to speak to him?'

Angel hadn't had time for the cat and had purposely not been in touch with Daniel Ashton about that diamond ring he very much liked.

'Yes, of course, put him through, please.'

There was a click and then a voice said, 'Is that Michael?'

'Hello, Daniel,' he said. 'Look Daniel, I am up to my neck in muck and bullets. I got your message, but I have this serial murder case on my lap and I have had to put thoughts of diamond rings absolutely on hold.'

Daniel said, 'That's all right, Michael. I know how it will be. It's in all the papers. Quickly, I have had a three-stone diamond ring brought in which is a bigger flash than the original one you saw and liked, and it is nearer your price.'

'No, Daniel, thank you. I like the solitaire best. Look, if or when I catch this killer, I'll be in touch.'

'Tell you what, Michael. You like a flutter, don't you? A bit more incentive. If you catch the killer *before* your wedding anniversary on 14 May, I'll do the solitaire you liked at your price, £500, and if you don't, it'll be £800. How about that?'

Angel smiled. That would be great. He reasoned that even if he didn't solve the case and had to pay £800, Daniel hadn't put a time of delivery on it, so Angel wouldn't be pressured finding the £300 difference on the dot. He hoped that Daniel would let him have the ring for 14 May, the date of the anniversary, and allow him a few weeks to get the difference together somehow.

'All right, Daniel, you're on.'

Angel had only happy memories of DI Ashton as he was known before he retired from the police. He replaced the phone.

He took out the brown envelope where he made his notes from his inside pocket and began to review his priorities. The most important outstanding matter was the interviewing of Dale Lunn, Felicity Lunn's husband. He reached out to the phone and summoned Ahmed.

There was a knock at the door and DS Carter put her head round. 'I'm with Trevor Crisp, sir. Can we come in?'

'Yes, of course, Flora. I was wondering where you two had got to.'

They were followed round the door by Ahmed.

Angel looked at Carter and Crisp. 'Hang on a minute,' he said. 'Sit down.'

Then he turned to Ahmed. 'Will you get me Dale Lunn's phone number, lad? Don Taylor may have it. Or it might be in the phone book.'

'Right, sir,' he said and he dashed out.

He looked over the desk at the two sergeants and said, 'Right, what have you got?'

They glanced at each other and then Crisp said, 'I, er, we didn't speak to anybody who had seen anything unusual, sir.'

Angel sighed.

Flora said, 'We inquired about newspaper deliveries and no one on Cemetery Road had papers delivered anymore. So I went to the post office and the manager of postal deliveries said that *that* walk was started at 8.10 a.m. yesterday which was way after the murder was committed.'

Angel wrinkled his nose. 'Yes, that's right. The murder was committed between 5 and 8 a.m. The murderer *could* have returned home, had a wash and gone back to bed.'

'That's assuming that . . .' Crisp began. 'Are you thinking that the murderer lives locally, sir?'

'Well, yes. Sebastopol Terrace, Monserrat Street and then Cemetery Road are the addresses of all three murders which are easily within a ten-minute walk of each other, aren't they?'

'So this murderer may not have a car,' Flora said.

Angel nodded. 'Probably has, but doesn't choose to use it. A knife, the cauliflower and the rice would easily fit in a plastic shopping bag or a carrier.'

There was a knock at the door.

Angel glared at it. There were far too many interruptions. 'Come in,' Angel said.

It was Ahmed. He had a slip of paper in his hand. He seemed surprised to see DS Crisp and DS Carter still there.

'That's that phone number you wanted, sir,' he said, passing Angel a page torn out of his notebook. He looked at the sergeants. 'Sorry to interrupt, sir.'

'Thank you, Ahmed,' Angel said, taking the slip of paper and stuffing it in his pocket.

Ahmed went out.

'Let's move on,' Angel said. 'We learn from the murderer's notes that he intends to kill six people. He has already killed three. It is therefore a matter of great urgency that we find him before he gets to the fourth. I fear that short of posting armed officers with every woman about sixty years of age who lives in Bromersley, the guarantee of their safety is unachievable.

'At this time, there is nothing more important than this investigation. We are trying to save lives. Do not get involved in any other case. If you have a problem with this with another member of staff, refer them to me. And if either of you think you have come across anything, phone me on my mobile. It is never switched off. Right. That's it. Off you go.'

Meanwhile, in his bedroom over the shop at 83 Sebastopol Terrace, Cliff Grant was hastily pulling up his trousers and tucking in his shirt as he could hear the shop door being hammered on so hard that he thought it might be knocked down if he didn't go down the stairs and open it. He pushed his feet into his slippers and rushed down. From the back of the chair in the kitchen, he snatched up the long blue overall his mother used to wear in the shop and shoved an arm in the sleeve as he made for the shop door.

He turned the sign round to read OPEN and turned the key.

A fat, irate old woman with a face like a bag of bones waddled in.

It was Mrs Beasley. She scowled at Grant and said, 'I thought this shop opened at eight o'clock, young man?'

Grant knew his mother would have had it open at eight o'clock even if it was in the middle of an earthquake. 'Well, I don't have a fixed time, really, Mrs Beasley. What can I get for you?' he said.

She wrinkled her nose.

Grant noticed for the first time that her nostrils were black and round, and her nose was short, like that of a pig.

'A bottle of vinegar,' she said. 'You can't eat chips without a good sozzling of vinegar.'

Grant put a bottle of vinegar in front of her. 'Twenty-nine pence,' he said.

She looked at it, sniffed and said, 'And summat for his breakfast.'

'What?' Grant said. 'Rice Krispies? Shredded Wheat? Muesli?'

'No. No. None of that muck,' she said as she gazed round the shop. 'How much is that tin of corned beef?'

Grant frowned and reached up to one of the high positions. He turned the tin all the way round, hoping that his mother had put a price on it. He was relieved to find that she had.

'Two pounds ninety-eight,' he said. He put it down on the counter in front of her. 'Anything else, Mrs Beasley?'

She looked at him, sniffed again and said, 'Not at these prices, Cliff. You know, I was very sorry to hear about your mother, but she was always far too dear, and it looks as if you're following in her footsteps.'

She tossed a five-pound note grudgingly onto the counter. Grant shook his head in dismay and rang up the money to put it in the till. 'If I could sell as much as Cheapo's, Mrs Beasley, I could be as cheap as Cheapo's.'

'None of your smart talk, Cliff. I've known you and your mother a long time. I wiped your backside when all you could do was bawl. And my goodness, could you bawl!'

He smiled at her. 'I never knew that,' he said, pushing her change towards her. 'Two pounds two pence. Thank you very much.'

She raked up the coins, then looked at him closely and with a serious expression said, 'There's a lot you don't know, Cliff Grant.'

The shop door opened and Maisie Spencer came in. She looked at Grant. He looked back at her. Her face was glowing. His heart missed a beat. They smiled at each other.

Mrs Beasley took one look at her, then at him and said, 'And you want to be careful of her, Cliff, for one thing. Give her half a chance and she'll eat you up and spit out the bones.'

Maisie Spencer's face went scarlet. 'Mind your own business, Mrs Beasley. What do *you* know?'

'Well, I know a helluva lot, Maisie Spencer. I know that I didn't have to rent it out at ten quid a time, like your Aunt Dolly did. I was straight up and down when I married my husband and we've been together for forty-two years. Had four children and brought them up proper. I've stuck it out through thick and bloody thin. And let me tell you, there's been more times thin than thick.' She made a gesture with two fingers, lifted her arm and said, 'So *up* yours.'

Maisie Spencer was so angry she could hardly speak. She snatched the handle of the shop door, yanked it open and said, 'Get out, you bleeding old trouble-maker.'

'I'm going, when I'm good and ready,' Mrs Beasley said.

Then she picked up the vinegar and the tin of corned beef from the counter and turned to Grant. 'I can see what's going on here with this tart, Cliff,' she said. 'And I have to say that your mother would *never* have approved. She would have wanted you to settle down with a decent lass, not a lass that's tried it on with just about every man on Canal Street.'

'You dirty, lying bitch!' Maisie Spencer said.

Mrs Beasley lifted up her head, turned and waddled towards the open door of the shop.

Her grand exit was spoiled by the arrival of Percy Maddison, the bread deliveryman. He usually delivered at that time and was trying to get to the counter, past Maisie Spencer and Mrs Beasley. He carried a large wooden tray of bread and cakes.

'Oh, sorry, madam,' Maddison said as he squeezed through. 'Excuse me.'

Mrs Beasley glared at the man. 'Get out of the bloody way, man,' she said, angrily pushing the tray out of her face. The front of it went up, the back went down and loaves of bread and cakes slid off the tray onto the floor of the shop.

'Stupid cow,' Maisie Spencer said.

Maddison turned back to her and said, 'Nay, missis, you didn't have to do *that*.'

Mrs Beasley ignored them all. With her nose raised high, she toddled out of the shop.

Grant's mouth was wide open. He was stumped at the behaviour of the women. He saw the mess of bread and cakes on the floor and said, 'I'll give you a hand, Percy.'

He lifted the flap in the gap in the counter and passed through to the customer side of the shop.

He saw that Maisie Spencer was standing against the wall. She had tears in her eyes, her hands up to her face and she was shaking.

He touched her gently on the arm. 'Why don't you go in the back, Maisie?' he said. 'I'll be through soon.'

She nodded and quietly slipped through the gap in the counter into the kitchen.

Maddison put the bread tray on the floor and the two men squatted together on their haunches close together. From that position, as they retrieved the loaves, tea-cakes and fancies, Maddison came very close to Grant's ear and in a confiding tone said, 'Women are the strangest of creatures, Cliff. You need to be very careful.'

Grant nodded. 'I'm trying to be,' he whispered.

Then at his usual volume, he said, 'Sorry about that, Percy. I don't know what gets into them.'

Maddison got to his feet and picked up the tray. 'Not your fault, Cliff,' he said. 'But I must say, you do have some funny customers round here.'

Maddison and Grant completed their business, Grant found himself obliged to buy more bread and cakes than he would normally have done, and the bread man left with a cheery, 'See you tomorrow, Cliff.'

Grant went into the kitchen and Maisie raced across to him and they embraced as if they hadn't seen each other for a month of Sundays.

When the passion eased and they rested from kissing, Grant said, 'Maisie, my love, while I am over the moon to see you, you can't stay. The shop bell can ring at any minute and I will simply *have* to answer it.'

The smile left her.

'Do you? Do you *really*?' she said. 'You could close the shop and lock the door.'

Grant sighed. 'Now you know I *can't* do that.'

She pouted her lips and ran her hands up and down his back. 'You can. Just for an hour or so. Go on,' she said.

He shook his head several times rapidly. 'No. This is *my* business now and I owe it to my mother to try to make a go of it.'

She licked her lips for a few seconds and said, 'Didn't last night mean *any*thing to you?'

He smiled. 'It was absolutely fabulous, Maisie.'

She giggled. 'Well, then . . .'

'I'll tell you what, Maisie,' he said. 'After I've closed the shop—' He broke off as the shop door opened and the bell rang.

'We *are* busy this morning,' he said. He gave her a peck on the cheek and turned to go.

She grabbed his hand and held him back. 'You *do* love me, don't you?' she said.

'Of course I love you,' he said quickly.

She released the grip and he dashed into the shop.

When he saw who was in the shop, his eyebrows shot up and his mouth dropped open. It was the dusky Ann Fiske dressed to the nines.

'Good morning, Cliff. Remember me?' she said.

He swallowed. She looked like a film star arriving at the Oscars ceremony.

'What's the matter, Cliff? Cat got your tongue? You look as if you've been caught with your fingers in the till.'

He detected something unfriendly in her attitude towards him.

'No, er . . . er Tutshy Face, not at all,' he said. He was certain that Maisie Spencer would be listening and he couldn't resist a quick glance in the direction of the kitchen. Shredded Wheat cartons blocked his view.

'It's lovely to see you,' he said. 'How's your father? Is he out of hospital?'

'Yes, he's home. It was a false alarm. He's fine for the moment.'

'That's great,' he said.

He was struggling to find things to say that were not controversial. 'Shouldn't you be at school, teaching the kiddywinks how to scrape their violins?' he said.

'I'm a peripatetic music teacher, Cliff. And I don't have a class on Friday mornings.'

'Oh. I didn't realize. Did you come for anything special?'

She breathed in smartly through her nose, raised it and said, 'Oh yes, as a matter of fact I did. A little bird told me that after you left me last night, you went visiting.'

Cliff heard the sound of a sharp intake of breath from behind him. It could only have come from Maisie Spencer.

He began to think that Ann Fiske knew more than she had said. His eyeballs slid sideways away from her and then back again. He licked the corners of his lips. He had better not deny it.

'Yes, I did,' he said. 'Why?'

'It was to *Miss* Spencer, wasn't it?' She said. 'Maisie Spencer.'

'It might have been. Where have you got all your information from? Have you got a private detective following me or something?'

'And that you stayed there a long time. How long did you actually stay, Cliff?'

'What is all this, Ann? I don't have people following *you* around,' he said.

'I don't have people following you, either. It was just that a friend of mine saw you. How long were you there, Cliff?'

'Well, er, she's a friend.'

Ann Fiske blinked. 'I thought *we* had an understanding.'

'Well, so we have.'

'It doesn't allow for *you* spending long evenings alone in the privacy of Maisie Spencer's home. Everybody knows she's "the tart with a heart".'

Cliff heard a further angry outburst of hot breath from behind the Shredded Wheat boxes. He bit his top lip and said, 'Well you have to be erm . . . erm . . . reasonable in this situation.'

That was too much for Ann Fiske. Her face went scarlet. '*Reasonable*?' she said. '*I* have never made promises of exclusive devotion to *you* and brought *you* chocolates, and then visited another man!'

And that was too much for Maisie Spencer. The Shredded Wheat boxes came to life.

'*Chocolates*,' she boomed as she came from behind them. She stood hands on hips, facing Grant and said, 'You've *never* brought *me* any chocolates.'

Ann Fiske gasped then glared at Maisie and said, 'You trollop. You rotten, little trollop. You've been listening to everything I've been saying.'

'Don't you *dare* call me names, Miss Iron Knickers. Just because you can't pull a man, there's no need to go around making rude remarks about those who *can*. Besides that, me and Cliff are engaged.'

Ann Fiske's eyes stood out like bilberries on stalks. '*Engaged*,' she roared. She turned to face Grant. 'Is this true?'

Grant blinked several times. His mouth opened as if to speak. Nothing came out. He coughed then said, 'Well, we'd been . . . er, talking about it.'

Maisie Spencer's turned to face him. '*Talking about it?*' she said. 'You bloody liar. You asked me to marry you over a year ago, before you went away.'

Ann Fiske said, 'Right, Maisie Spencer, where's the ring? Hold up your hand. Show me the engagement ring.'

'He never bought me a ring,' Maisie said.

Ann Fiske smiled. But there wasn't any warmth in it. 'No,' she said, 'and he *never* will.' Then she looked fiercely at Grant and said, 'Because he's *no* good. My father said *that* after he first met him. He knew *his* father, Philip Grant. He was another right conman. I came here this morning hoping for an explanation I could live with. I would almost certainly have made it up with him, but what I know now there is no chance of that.'

Grant was overwhelmed by them, but he had to try and rescue his reputation.

'Ann,' he said, 'I couldn't buy her a decent ring because I couldn't afford to. I didn't have a bean until Ma died.' Then he turned to Maisie Spencer and said, 'Don't listen to her. I've *promised* you a ring and I will *get* you a ring.'

'You must have said that a hundred times,' Maisie said.

'And I meant it every time I said it,' he said.

Ann Fiske said, 'Well, I'll have to go. I'm fed up of listening to your lies and excuses.' She looked at Maisie Spencer and said, 'Are you coming or are you going to wait until he talks you into bed?'

'Huh! It'll be a long time before he talks *me* into any bed,' she said.

Maisie Spencer pushed past Grant, lifted the flap in the counter and squeezed through the gap, and the two young women swept out into the street, banging the shop door noisily behind them.

Grant's eyes, unblinking, stared at the closed door. He clenched his teeth. His face went scarlet. He turned and punched the stack of boxes of Shredded Wheat piled up against the side of the wall. They scattered across the floor of the shop. Then he went into the kitchen, violently kicking the boxes that had fallen in his way. He went to the settee, slumped heavily onto it, leaned down to the side and picked out a can of Monty's lager from an open pack, grabbed the ring, tore off the seal and took a long swig of lager. He swivelled round to put his head on one arm of the settee and his legs over the other, then he put the can back to his lips, emptied it and threw it powerfully at the sink. It hit the teapot standing at the edge of the draining board, which rolled off and smashed onto the kitchen floor.

NINE

Angel made contact with Mr Dale Lunn, husband of the late Felicity Lunn, and arranged to meet him at his house, 62 Cemetery Road at 9.30 that Friday morning.

Angel asked him the usual routine questions, but Mr Lunn was unable to tell him anything that progressed his inquiries. So Angel arranged for Lunn and his daughter to call in at the SOCs' office to have their fingerprints taken for elimination purposes. He then took his leave and hastily returned to his own office at the police station.

He was not a happy man. It was 12.30 and he felt that he had wasted an entire morning. He quickly phoned for Scrivens and set him on checking on Lunn's alibi, then he spoke to Don Taylor and asked him if there had been any fresh developments from the previous day's forensic investigations in the Felicity Lunn case. He was thinking in particular of the vacuuming of the SOC, and the rest of the house; also the contents of the waste bins. However, Taylor's reply to both questions was in the negative.

Angel replaced the receiver, sighed heavily and promptly returned to his notes. He was checking to see that he had not overlooked anything.

He noticed that regarding the appeal that had had front page coverage in most national papers, up to five-minute pieces on television news and shorter reports on the radio, no 60-year-old women who knew any of the three victims had come forward. Angel regarded that as very bad news. It was making it easy for the murderer to continue her evil activities.

The phone rang. He reached out for it. It was Detective Superintendent Harker. Angel's face dropped as he expected the superintendent was to send him out on another cauliflower and rice murder.

'Angel? Come up here,' Harker said.

'Right, sir,' Angel said.

He put the phone back in its cradle. He began wondering what Harker could be wanting to see him about. It was a relief that it wasn't another cauliflower and rice murder. That would have been far too urgent for any discussion at this stage. However, it was never for anything helpful and it was never to approve of anything he had done or said. He knew that whatever it was, he would need to have a hide as thick as a Centurion Tank and the feelings of a gnat to survive the old warrior.

He trudged up the green corridor to the superintendent's office and knocked on the door.

Amidst a bout of coughing Harker said, 'Come in. Sit down.'

Harker's office as usual smelled of a mixture of TCP and Fennings Fever Cure and was predictably as hot as Death Valley.

Harker was seated at his desk. He was a skinny, small man. His bald head, with taxi door ears, was the shape of a turnip. The small amount of hair left to him by parsimonious living was a mixture of ginger, orange and white. His large desk was a jumble of piled up files, papers, letters, telephones, Kleenex, and boxes of different medications, including Movicol, paracetamol, and Co-codamol.

Angel noticed also that immediately in front of Harker was a pile of newspapers.

Harker sniffed, looked down at them and said, 'Made quite a name for yourself again, Angel, I see?'

Angel didn't attempt to take the bait.

Eventually Harker said, 'What was the motive in promoting such far-reaching publicity for a murderer who is quite obviously a local man?'

'I didn't need such *extensive* coverage, sir. But I did need *intensive* coverage, and I have no control over the boundaries the media covers. I needed to tell every woman in South Yorkshire who is around sixty years of age to try to remember the three women victims and if they knew them to come to the police for protection.'

'And how many have come forward?'

'None so far, sir. But it isn't twenty-four hours since I made the appeal.'

'The TV news and radio programmes were reporting it last night. All the tabloids ran with it on the front page and the broadsheets had pieces inside. If there had been any people out there who could have filled your requirements, they would have come forward, so clearly the plan failed.'

'It's very early to reach that judgement, sir.'

'It certainly isn't.'

'It is only one o'clock on the day of publication. Many people won't even have read their newspaper yet.'

'Those who didn't see the television news, listen to their radio last night and this morning and haven't even glanced at the front page of a newspaper will be very few people indeed.'

Angel shrugged. He could be right, but he hoped he wasn't.

'I suppose it has dawned on you that all three murders were executed between 5 and 8 a.m. What does that signify to you?'

'That the murderer wants to make it difficult for us to establish alibis, sir,' Angel said. 'Most people are in bed at that time. Many of them on their own. It probably simply means that that's the only time convenient.'

Harker nodded. 'What line of inquiry are you pursuing now?'

'We are delving into the history of the three victims to find out what is common to them all.'

'And where do you hope that that will lead?'

'I am hoping that whatever is common to those three will also be common to the remaining three, which should reveal the murderer.'

'Sounds to me that you are depending on luck and providence rather than a sensible, thought-out plan.'

'I assure you, sir, it is a very well-thought-out plan.'

'You have witnesses who have seen a peculiar woman with grey hair in a sheepskin coat in or near to two of the scenes. Why have you not pursued that?'

'I have, sir. A standard question to all people close to the victims has been, "have you seen anybody unusual around about the time of the murder?" And the answers — except for two witnesses — were "no". We have not broadened the public search because the description is so general and because the witnesses described the person differently. One said "strange-looking" and the other said "queer-looking" and I have not been able to reconcile that part of the description. All I've got that is common to both is "woman", "grey hair" and "long sheepskin coat". I simply didn't think it was sufficient to try and find a suspect on the strength of that alone. I was hoping that that information would be confirmed when we finally make an arrest.'

Harker wasn't favourably impressed. He looked as if the smell of the gravy in the cook house at Strangeways had just reached his nostrils.

'It seems to me that you are totally dependent on good luck, Angel. I thought *that* about your major strategy. And as for yesterday's time-wasting exercise with the national news media, it seems to me that you are seeking to cast yourself as some sort of detective supremo, the see-all, know-all and cure-all of everything criminal. This self-aggrandizement will not be appreciated by the Home Office.'

That stung Angel hard, even though over the years, he had tolerated all kinds of similar insults from Harker.

However, he kept his cool. 'Perhaps their opinion will change, sir,' he said, 'if I am able to catch this murderer.'

Harker shook his head and smiled. His smile was unusual . . . *and* rare. Angel saw it. It was enough to make a pig sick.

'Angel,' Harker said. 'You've about as much chance of catching this murderer as you have of winning the lottery.'

Angel shrugged off the insult. Anyway, it did not apply to him. He didn't buy lottery tickets.

It was 4.45 on Friday afternoon, 8 May. Angel was glancing through the post to see that nothing important was being neglected while he was fully occupied with the cauliflower and rice murders, when there was a knock at the door.

'Come in,' he called.

It was Ahmed. He did not seem to be his usual joyful self. He looked very serious. 'Can I talk to you, sir? It's not about the case.'

'Of course you can, lad. I know it's a bit of a madhouse, but if it's important I hope you know you can always talk to me. Now . . . sit down. What is it about?'

'Well, sir, I've had a phone call from Mrs Kenworthy, the Chief Constable's . . . er, secretary.'

Angel looked at the young man. 'Yes?' Angel said.

'I've never spoken to her before, sir. I've seen her many a time . . . but if you pass her in the corridor or anywhere she looks the other way.'

'Well, she thinks she's important, Ahmed. Don't worry about her. She does the same thing to me. She never nods or smiles or invites conversation. So what?'

'Well, sir, she said on the phone that the Chief Constable's away, that he returns on Wednesday 13 May, and that he wants to see me in his office at ten o'clock next Thursday morning. I asked her what for and she said she was not at liberty to say and that it was a confidential matter.'

Angel frowned, gently rubbed his chin and said, 'Yes, so what?'

'Well, sir, I can't think what he wants. He knows all there is to know about me. There's nothing confidential I can think of. Has anybody been complaining about me or something?'

Angel sighed. 'I'm sure I don't know, Ahmed, but it is probably nothing at all. It could be that somebody has said something *good* about you. Had you thought about that?'

At that, Ahmed gave Angel a huge smile, and Angel had to smile back at him.

'If I were you, I'd get my haircut, and on that Thursday, I'd press my best suit and come in it. The Chief will appreciate that, and it will give you confidence. Then, whether it is trouble, something mundane or something really nice, you would be suitably dressed.'

Ahmed lowered his eyes and shook his head. 'But what if he doesn't think I'm suitable to be in the force and he wants me out?'

Angel's eyes opened wide. 'It'll be nothing like that, Ahmed. I should just be patient and wait. Think happy thoughts. I'm sure it will be all right.'

He looked up. 'Do you really think so, sir?'

'I do,' Angel said. 'It's always best to be an optimist, Ahmed. Now push off, there's a good lad. I've a lot on my plate.'

Ahmed got to his feet.

There was a knock at the door.

'Come in,' Angel called.

It was DC Scrivens. He looked at Ahmed and then back at Angel. 'Oh, are you busy, sir?'

'Ahmed's just going,' Angel said.

Ahmed looked at Angel and said, 'Thanks very much, sir.'

Angel gave him a reassuring smile and a nod, then Ahmed went out and closed the door.

Angel turned back to Scrivens and said, 'Now then, Ted, what is it?'

'I've finished checking on Dale Lunn's alibi, sir.'

Angel's eyebrows shot up. 'That was quick.'

Scrivens said he had been to the Corporation Bus depot and spoken to the general manager who had confirmed that Lunn was on route 63 that Wednesday night/Thursday morning, in addition, the night cashier who checked Lunn's money satchel that Thursday morning gave Scrivens the times that were recorded on Lunn's receipt and in the company's log book. Angel found that everything matched exactly with the report Lunn had made to him. So that clearly made it impossible for him to have murdered his wife.

Angel thanked him. Scrivens smiled and went out.

Angel looked at his watch. It said five o'clock. He rubbed his chin . . . wrinkled his nose and reached for his hat. It had been far from a perfect day.

Angel didn't like working Saturdays (and Mary didn't like him working on Saturdays either) but sometimes it had to be done.

He arrived at his office at 8.28 on the button, as if it were a weekday. He knew that there would be no Ahmed to run about for him. CID, including SOCO, was virtually closed down out of hours except for serious cases. The uniformed division operated seven days a week, but there were fewer officers on duty, unless there was something special happening such as a home football match. The vehicle unit, however, was always on patrol, monitoring a section of the M1 as well as selected roads and streets in the Bromersley area where motorists might be tempted to exceed the speed limit or break the law in other ways.

Angel took out the pocket recording machine and was considering starting the playback when there was an unexpected knock on the door.

'Come in,' he said.

It was DS Crisp and DS Carter. They didn't look overjoyed, either.

'Good morning, sir,' they said.

'Come in. Come in. Sit down. Have you both completed your interviews? Did you manage to get any old friends or a relation who was older than the victim?'

'Well, sir,' Flora said. 'I—'

The phone rang.

Angel glared at it, then looked at Flora. 'Sorry, lass. Just hold what you were going to say.'

He snatched up the phone. 'Angel,' he said.

'It's DS Clifton, sir. I saw that you were in the building. I've just had a triple nine. A woman by the name of Michele Pulman, has been found dead, reported by her daily help, Emily Cole.'

Angel's hand went to his head. His pulse raced. 'Oh no,' he said. 'Not another.' His chest tightened.

He looked at Trevor and Flora. They looked back at him. They could see it was serious. He sighed. Then snatched up a pen.

'Give me the address, Bernie,' Angel said into the phone.

'13 Creesford Road, sir.'

'Bernie, will you notify SOC, Dr Mac and the duty officer?'

'Right, sir.'

'And have you got the phone number?'

Clifton gave Angel the number.

Angel replaced the phone, turned to Trevor Crisp and Flora Carter and gave them the news. They both expressed their dismay at another suspected murder. Angel directed them to divide the house numbers on Creesford Road between them and begin the house to house. They rushed off.

He tapped in the phone number DS Clifton had given him and then took out a brown envelope from his inside pocket and a ballpoint pen to make notes. The phone rang out a long time before it was answered and then nobody spoke.

Angel could hear quick, soft breathing.

'Is this the home of Michele Pulman?' he said.

There was still no reply.

'This is the police,' he said. 'Is this Miss Emily Cole?'

'Oh yes,' a small, polite voice said. 'I'm sorry but er . . . I am not used to er . . . Hello?'

'Miss Cole, don't worry,' Angel said. 'A doctor and the police are on the way. Are *you* all right?'

'Oh, yes, thank you. However, I will be relieved to hand over the responsibility for Mrs Pulman to them.'

'Of course, of course,' he said. 'Please don't touch anything or move anything, will you?'

'Oh no. I am afraid that I have, I used the phone to report the . . .'

'That will be all right, Miss Cole, but please don't touch or move anything else. While you are waiting, perhaps you could help me with some information?'

'I will try,' she said.

'Why do you believe that Mrs Pulman is dead?'

'Well . . . oh dear . . . well, her chest is covered in blood, she has no pulse and she is not breathing . . . oh dear . . . also . . . also she seems to have choked on uncooked rice. Although I have absolutely no idea how she came by it. In fact, I don't think she liked rice.'

Angel sighed heavily. He rubbed his temple for a few seconds. 'I suppose that there is a cauliflower on her stomach?' he said slowly.

There was a long pause. He wondered what was happening. Eventually Emily Cole said, 'How could you possibly know that?'

'We are looking for a psychopath, Miss Cole. One who kills because he or she likes killing. The killer has killed three times before. The victims were women aged around sixty or thereabouts. We know about the cauliflower because it was part of the MO.'

'Oooooh,' she said. 'Mrs Pulman has just had a birthday. She was sixty-one.'

He nodded. It was no surprise, just more unnecessary corroboration.

'Will you tell me how you came to find Mrs Pulman in this state?'

'I am Mrs Pulman's carer. I called as I usually call, every day at about 8.15 to wash her, change her and give her breakfast. I have a key and I let myself in. She's usually asleep and I have to wake her up. I didn't notice anything different about the house until I came in here and saw her sitting up in bed, her head in a strange position, her cheeks bloated and all that blood . . . I went up close to her and picked up her wrist to see if there was a pulse, and there wasn't. Her mouth fell open, some rice dropped out . . . and I saw all that rice round her teeth and gums. So I knew she had gone and that I had to phone the police.'

Angel bit his lip and said, 'Sorry to put you through that, Miss Cole.'

'I'm stronger than I look, sir,' she said, then she added, 'I had forgotten, you can't see me.'

Angel smiled. 'No, but I can visualize you. Did you notice if anything in the house has been stolen . . . anything at all?'

'No. But I hadn't thought about it . . . I must have a look round . . .'

'And has anything been left by the murderer?'

'I haven't noticed, and I would know if there was anything.'

'If you do notice anything *after* Scenes of Crime have made their checks, do please come forward and tell us, won't you?'

'I certainly will.'

'That's good. Thank you,' Angel said. 'And by the by, what relation are you to Mrs Pulman?'

'Well, I am — I looked after her. I was her friend. I was also her paid carer and I ran her house for her.'

'Did you sleep in?'

'No. Perhaps I should have done. I came every day, usually twice, but sometimes more. She was bed-bound, you see. Every day, I did what was necessary. Two or three hours, sometimes up to six hours. I've been doing it for eight years.'

'Whereabouts do you live?'

'I'm not far away. Six Orchard Grove. Across the road. Third house down on the left. You can reach me on the phone, Bromersley 249322.'

'Thank you. I'm just writing it down, Miss Cole,' he said. 'And how old are you?'

'I'm seventy-two. But don't think that I was too old to be capable of looking after Mrs Pulman and running two households.'

'You sound much younger, Miss Cole, and I don't doubt your capabilities for one moment. Do you happen to know Mrs Pulman's next of kin?'

'That would be her cousin in Canada, I believe. But she hasn't seen her for many years.'

'Isn't there anybody nearer? Isn't there a husband and children?'

'Oh no,' she said. 'I understand that she had been married and had a daughter, but they both died, some years ago.'

'Does she have a solicitor?'

'Yes,' she said. 'Barnes and Barnes on Victoria Road.'

'Thank you,' he said. 'Have you any idea of anybody who would wish Mrs Pulman any harm?'

'Certainly not. She was a very good-living, charming and beautiful woman. I'm not aware that she had an enemy in the world.'

'Well, who would benefit from her death? I assume she has left a Will.'

'Ooooh, I have no idea. I know *I* don't. I've lost a dear friend and I'm out of a job. That's all I know.'

Then through the phone, Angel heard a loud banging. It sounded like someone knocking on a door.

'Excuse me,' Miss Cole said. 'I think your men have arrived. Hold on, please.'

Through the earpiece, Angel heard the door being unlocked, opened, a distant male voice talking to Miss Cole and then her reply. That was followed by several other voices. Seconds later she came back to the phone.

'Hello,' she said. 'Are you there? Yes, they *are* policemen.'

'I'm assuming they are the men from the Scenes of Crimes Office, Miss Cole? Can I speak to DS Taylor?'

'I'll ask,' she said.

Moments later Taylor came onto the phone. 'Is that you, sir?'

'I have already found out that the MO is as before, Don,' Angel said. 'Would you check that there is a note on the victim's chest? And if there is, read it out to me.'

'Right, sir,' Taylor said. 'Hold on. It'll take a little while.'

Angel waited. He used the time to re-read his notes and make any hastily written unclear words comprehensible.

Taylor came back to the phone. 'Yes, it's the same MO, sir. The note is folded the same. As the lady was dressed in night attire, it was shoved down the neck of her nightdress, sticking out so that it could be seen. I had the victim photographed before taking it out, so that you will be able to see exactly how it was.'

'Thank you, Don. Read it out.'

There was the crinkle of the paper being unfolded.

Taylor said, 'It says:

Michele Pulman was unfaithful, that is why,

In spite of her beauty, she had to die.

Michele is the fourth, and there are two more to go.'

Angel rapidly scribbled it down.

He winced when Taylor read out the last line.

'Thank you, Don,' he said. 'Goodbye.'

He replaced the phone.

Angel read it again silently then rested his hand on his chin and closed his eyes. He was thinking . . . the note was about a relationship or more than one relationship. It said she was murdered because she was "unfaithful". The notes left on the other women were also criticisms of their natures. Gladys Grant was "a vicious bitch", Fay Hough was "self-willed", and Felicity Lunn was "too much fun, nasty and dirty".

Was the murderer writing about the relationships the women had with her father, he wondered? With psychopaths, as with many criminals, their moral parameters become confused. Rampton was full of people who were perfectly normal most of the time, but there was a kink in their genetic make-up that from time to time caused them to commit the most horrendous crimes while instantly returning apparently to their usual amiable natures. Standards are very low among some families and communities in this post religious society, Angel thought.

He was further ruminating about low moral standards when he heard a distant church clock strike ten o'clock. It arrested his thoughts. This wasn't the time for idle meditation. He could do that while shaving, watching wordy repeats on television or when he couldn't sleep. He looked down at the notes he had made while interviewing Emily Cole. There were matters he couldn't deal with in a few minutes on a Saturday morning. He wondered if Barnes and Barnes, the victim's solicitors, would be accessible. He pulled out the telephone directory, found the number and tapped it on to the phone keypad.

The phone was answered by a man. 'Hello, Barnes and Barnes,' he said.

'This is DI Angel of Bromersley Police. Who am I speaking to?'

'Gerard Barnes, Inspector. We are closed actually. I'm the only one here, but if I can help you, I will.'

'Thank you, Mr Barnes. I do hope you can. A woman, a Mrs Michele Pulman has been found murdered this morning. I need some information about her next of kin, her husband, and I believe she also had a child. And I need to have a copy of her Will. I want to know who would benefit from her death.'

'Oh dear. Very sorry to hear that. Poor dear lady. She was a very wealthy woman who has had more of her share of bad luck,' Barnes said. 'Yes, we represent her. I was with her only a couple of weeks ago. Excuse me while I find her file . . . Here we are. Let me see . . . Yes, her next of kin is Mrs Jessica Loring, 446 Maple Avenue, Ontario 120987878.'

'Thank you,' Angel said scribbling away. 'Do you have her phone number, Mr Barnes, by any chance?'

'No. I'm sorry, we don't. Now her Will would need to be copied, Inspector. The earliest I can do that is when I have some staff here. That would be Monday morning. You could have it collected then or we could post it on to you.'

'I will send somebody to collect it on Monday morning, if that is convenient to you, Mr Barnes.'

'I'll see that it is prepared first thing, Inspector.'

'Thank you, and can you help me with the whereabouts of her husband and child?'

'No, I'm afraid I can't. I think that they both died a long while back, but I can't be sure when.'

Angel thanked him and ended the call.

He sat back in the chair and thought about the quickest, most reliable way of finding out what happened to Michele Pulman's husband and child. He pulled open the middle drawer of his desk and took out a copy of the International Police Directory. He found the overseas telephone number for the Ontario Provincial Police, (*Police Provinciale de l'Ontario*), and he tapped it into his phone.

He was soon speaking to the Captain of the Mounties in Ontario. Reception was as clear as if he had been speaking to Mary at home.

Angel explained the problem and the captain said he was delighted to assist the British Police. He said that he would verify that the address was valid and check whether anything criminal was known about the residents. He kept Angel waiting several minutes then he came back and said that the address *was* valid and nothing criminal was associated with the residents. Angel then asked the captain if he could supply him with the telephone number of the house. He certainly could and a few moments later rattled out the number.

Angel was delighted. He thanked the captain profusely for his information and time, and ended the call.

He looked at his watch. It was eleven o'clock. He wondered if Mac, Don Taylor. Trevor Crisp or Flora Carter had uncovered anything new or different in their numerous and diverse searches. They could have. But then again, it could be just so much time-wasting nonsense.

He fished into his pocket and took out his mobile. He checked that it was switched on then he put it back into his pocket. He had wanted to satisfy himself that they could contact him if the need arose.

Picking up the landline phone, he dialled the long Canadian telephone number.

It rang a long time and then a woman's voice cheerily said, 'Hello. Jessica Loring speaking.'

Angel was pleased to make contact so easily. She came through as clear as a bell.

'Mrs Loring,' he said. 'I'm Inspector Angel, a police officer speaking to you from Bromersley in England.'

There was a slight pause. Her voice changed and she said, 'Oh dear. It's about Michele, isn't it? What's happened?'

'I'm afraid so, Mrs Loring. Michele died very early this morning.'

'Oh dear. Well, it was to be expected, I suppose. She has been ill for years. It will have come to her as a blessing, I expect.'

'I'm sorry to have to break this news to you and then ask questions but that's my job. Mrs Pulman's solicitor told me that you were her next of kin, and that you would be able to tell me about her husband and daughter.'

'Well they're both dead, Inspector. Died ten years ago now. I never met them, but of course Michele told me about them in her letters. We used to exchange newsy letters years ago. Lately, we just put much shorter notes in cards on birthdays and at Christmas and so on.'

'Do you know their exact names in full and where and when they died?'

'I know that it was in a road accident, and that they both died. I can't remember the date. He was called Dominic and their daughter, who was twenty years old, was Annabelle.'

'Thank you very much, Mrs Loring. There's just one more thing. What was Michele's maiden name?'

'Noble, Inspector. She was Michele Noble.'

'Thank you, Mrs Loring. Thank you very much.'

'You didn't tell me, Inspector. The cause of Michele's passing?'

He bit his lip, sighed and said, 'No, I didn't, Mrs Loring. I didn't want to upset you. We believe that she has three wounds in her heart made with a knife.'

'Oh! Oh!' he heard her cry out. 'How dreadful. How absolutely dreadful. Oh dear. Have you caught the person who has done it?'

'No. I am hopeful that the information you have given me will assist with the investigation.'

Mrs Loring hesitated, then she said, 'I don't see how. It certainly wasn't her husband or their daughter.'

'We are looking for a serial killer, Mrs Loring. Mrs Pulman is the fourth victim. It is very difficult. Do you know of anybody who would have wished Michele any harm?'

'Certainly not. I wouldn't have thought anybody would have thought badly about her. She hadn't a wicked bone in her body.'

'Well, thank you very much, Mrs Loring. I'm sorry I was the bearer of such tragic news. Please accept my sincere condolences.'

He managed to end the interview without causing more distress and he returned the phone to its cradle.

He rubbed his chin. Finding out what happened to the husband and the daughter was something that must be investigated. He would set Ahmed on searching records first thing on Monday morning.

He made a note on his envelope.

The phone began to ring. Angel threw down his pen and reached out for it. He saw from the LCD it was Dr Mac. He assumed he was ringing from Michele Pulman's house.

'Yes, Mac. What is it?'

'Is that you, Michael Angel? I'll tell ye, I don't reckon much to being hauled out of bed at this god-forsaken time on a Saturday morning. Why can't your murderers work a five-day week? And why does this one have to kill so early in the day? It's aboot time you caught the bastard and got him put away.'

Angel said, 'You irritable, mean and cynical old man. Don't you—'

'Nae so much of the old. You'll be my age one day.'

'Not for fifty or sixty years,' Angel said with a grin. 'And if I make it, I bet you I'll not be half as miserable as you.'

'It's all right for you. You're happy to sit at home with the ever-patient Mary and watch repeats of *Bad Girls* on the telly. I had planned to catch a salmon or two off Filey Brigg.'

'You'll still have time to get there, sit in the rain, get bored out of your head and catch pneumonia. Have you rung up just to gripe or do you have any information for me?'

'I have just said what was on my mind, ye ken.'

'You know what I need to know, Mac.'

'Have you a pen ready?'

'The ink's probably dried up with waiting for you. Yes. Fire ahead.'

'All right, well, I could say ditto really. The cause of death *apparently* (and to be confirmed) is loss of blood due to stabbing three times in the heart, the time of death was between five and eight this morning, and the mouth and gullet was rammed full of ordinary, uncooked, dried rice and she has a cauliflower in her lap. From memory, Michael, that's exactly the same as the other three. That's why I could have said ditto. And that's all I've got until Monday morning when I will get her on the slab.'

'Thanks, Mac,' Angel said, as he considered the details the doctor had rattled off to him.

'Will any of that help you, Michael?'

'It's too early to say. It's useful to know that she was almost certainly murdered by the same psychopath as the other three. You would have told me if you had observed anything unusual about the crime scene, wouldn't you?'

'I would, and there wasn't. Same wounds, same cauliflower, same rice and the same boring blood.'

'Right, Mac, thank you.'

'You're welcome. I need you to see the body and give me the nod to take it.'

'Of course. Will you put me on to Don Taylor?'

'Aye. He's here. Hold on.'

Mac passed over the phone.

'DS Taylor, sir.'

'Ah Don, I wonder if we've spent enough time looking at the rice and the cauliflowers. When you have time, would you take a look at the rice from each of the four victims and see if it is the same in all four cases. That is to say that it came — as far as you can tell — out of the same packet or batch. And the cauliflowers . . . is there anything to indicate their source? You know what I mean.'

'I *will* have a close look, sir, but generally — to me — rice is rice and a cauli is a cauli.'

'I know. I know. But I'm clutching at straws, here, Don.'

'I'll get back to you on that, sir.'

'Very good. Now, are you ready for me yet?' Angel said. 'I think Mac wants to get away.'

'By the time you get here, sir, we will be. By the way, I want the old woman, Miss Cole, back now. I need her prints for elimination. You have her address, sir.'

'I also have her phone number,' he said. 'Take this down. It's Bromersley 249322. I'll be with you in a very few minutes.'

TEN

It was half past eleven when Angel arrived at 13 Creesford Road. He parked the BMW behind Mac's car and walked along the drive of the elegant, architect-designed house, built during the excesses of the 1920s.

The uniformed policeman on the front door saluted him. Angel acknowledged the salute, opened the door and went in.

Taylor heard the door close and came out of the front room into the hall, still covered from head to toe in his sterile white overalls. He looked at Angel, pulled down his mask and said, 'Perfect timing, sir. Through here.'

Angel followed him back into the room. It was a large, well-furnished drawing room with the addition of a bed and bedside cabinets.

Mac was by the door. He had discarded his white overalls and was standing with his bag at his feet. There were two other SOC officers in whites: one was taking photographs and the other packing up a white valise with plastic boxes, some containing samples from the scene.

Sitting up in the bed, supported by pillows, Angel saw the body of a woman in a white nightdress. He crossed the room and went up close to the bed. Her eyes were closed. Her hair was jet black, her cheekbones were uncommonly high and pronounced. Even her hands were shapely and her nails perfectly manicured and glossed. He thought that when she was alive, she must have been strikingly beautiful.

Looking downwards to her lap was a mess of blood spattered over the nightdress and a cauliflower.

Angel turned to Taylor and said, 'Have you spotted anything here that is unusual or different from the other three murders?'

Taylor pursed his lips. 'No, sir,' he said. 'Tediously identical, I would say.'

Dr Mac coughed and said, 'You've already had my answer to that one, Michael. Is there any chance I could have the body?'

Angel identified a touch of tetchiness in the question. 'Of course, Mac,' he said.

Mac dived into his pocket, pulled out his mobile, clicked on a number, put the phone to his ear and ambled to the other end of the room.

The front door suddenly closed with a bang and was followed by a knock on the drawing room door which was ajar. Emily Cole came in. She looked round at the policemen one by one. Then she picked out DS Taylor, went up to him and said, 'Somebody phoned and asked me to see you about taking my fingerprints.'

Taylor said, 'That's right, Miss Cole. Won't keep you.'

She looked at him gently and said, 'While I am waiting, do you think I could have a minute with my friend, Mrs Pulman?' she said.

Taylor frowned. He wasn't sure what she meant.

Angel stepped forward and said, 'Of course you can, Miss Cole. You mustn't touch her, though.'

Miss Cole nodded her understanding, then turned back to Angel and said, 'I recognize your voice. You're the gentleman who spoke to me on the phone earlier, aren't you?'

He nodded. 'My name is Inspector Angel.'

'Thank you, Inspector,' she said. 'I just want to look at her and say my goodbyes.'

Angel walked with her up to the side of the bed. They stood, side by side.

Miss Cole first looked at the dead woman's face.

'Isn't she beautiful?' she said. 'I used to wash and set her hair every week. Not a grey hair in sight at 61, incredible, isn't it? There was nothing like doing her hair to cheer her up.'

Angel nodded.

'Look at her hands, Inspector. Aren't they a lovely shape? I used to give her a manicure every—'

She broke off. Her eyes flashed. She pointed to Mrs Pulman's hand and turned back to Angel.

'Her ring, Inspector,' she said. 'She's not wearing her ring. It was never off her finger. She wore it all the time. It was given to her by her husband.'

Angel's eyebrows shot up.

Emily Cole snatched open the drawer in the bedside table. Inside there were several boxes of pills. She picked them all out of the drawer as well as the white paper lining, but there was no ring. She threw the stuff back and slammed the drawer shut. Then she went down on her knees and looked under the bed.

Angel rubbed his chin. 'She could have taken it off,' he said.

'No. No. She was very sentimental about it. If she took it off, she would soon have put it back on again. Come to think, it was getting a bit loose for her. It sometimes used to swivel round.'

Angel turned to Taylor and said, 'Do you know anything about a ring, Don?'

'No, sir. I don't think she was wearing a ring.'

'You should have pics of the victim and scene taken on arrival?'

'We have, sir. We have. I'll get them up on a laptop. Won't take a sec.'

'Yes. Do that,' Angel said.

Taylor passed a laptop to the SOCO who had been taking photographs and muttered a few words. The man took the laptop and the camera and went out of the room.

Emily Cole's mind seemed to be wholly on the ring. Her face looked pained and thoughtful. As she stood up she said, 'It might be under her pillow. Can we get her out of bed?'

'Not until she is moved to the mortuary,' Angel said. 'The doctor will be having her collected shortly.'

Mac heard this, stepped forward and said, 'The mortuary van is on its way, Michael. Should be here in a few minutes.'

Angel nodded towards Mac, then turned to the old lady and said, 'Is there anything else missing, Miss Cole?'

Her face suddenly changed for the worse. Her eyes opened wide. '*Not* the Georgian silver tea set!' she said. Then she dashed out of the drawing room into the hall.

Angel signalled to Taylor with his thumb to follow her. She went out of the hall into the room next to it, the dining room. She stormed straight up to a big mahogany sideboard, pulled open one of the doors and dropped down on her knees again. Taylor squatted down beside her. She poked about inside for a few seconds then sighed, smiled and closed the sideboard cupboard door.

Taylor said, 'Is it there?'

She nodded and wearily got to her feet. 'All five pieces. Thank goodness,' she said.

They returned to the drawing room and Taylor reported that all was well.

'Are there any other treasures that might have been taken, Miss Cole?' Angel said.

She pulled back her head, stared at him in disbelief and said, 'The house is full of Mrs Pulman's treasures, Inspector. Keepsakes and things that reminded her of the past. I cannot possibly tell you that without giving it some thought . . . and having a good look round.'

'I realize that. I really meant in the way of money or gold or silver or Rembrandts or Picassos? Whatever it might be, it is important. We need to know about it.'

The SOC man came back with the laptop. He came straight to Angel and showed him the screen. 'Is that what you wanted, sir?' he said.

Angel glanced at it. 'Thank you,' he said and he took the laptop. Then he added, 'Miss Cole, will you come and look at this?'

It was a close-up photograph of Michele Pulman's midriff showing blood on the white nightdress and over a cauliflower. The backs of both of her hands were positioned under her bosom resting on her body. In the right-hand bottom corner of the photograph were the figures 9.06. 9.5.2015.

Angel looked at Miss Cole and said, 'The first digits of that figure on the picture is the time the photograph was taken. Six minutes past nine. So this was one of the earliest photographs taken here this morning. The time and date cannot be changed. The evidence therefore is unarguable. Mrs Pulman was not wearing a ring then.'

Miss Cole wrinkled up her nose then nodded. 'I have to accept that, Inspector,' she said.

Angel smiled then said, 'You'd better give me a description of that ring though, so that we can circulate it.'

'Yes,' she said. 'Well, it was two big-ish diamonds, offset in a claw setting with scroll work round the head. The ring was all platinum. It was very striking. Mrs Pulman said that the two stones represented her and her husband.'

Angel put the description on the back of the envelope. 'That's great,' he said. 'You know, Miss Cole, a photograph would be much better. Is there a photograph of Mrs Pulman wearing it, that we can blow up?'

'There's bound to be,' Miss Cole said. Then she put the fingers of one hand to the corner of her mouth as she thought. After a few moments, she held up one finger and marched towards the room door. Angel followed. She went out to the hall and into the dining room. She crossed to the huge sideboard and went straight down on her knees and pulled open a drawer, she fished inside it and eventually took out an old cardboard shoe box. She lifted the lid and it was filled with photographs.

She handed the box to Angel with a cherubic smile.

'I expect there will be one in there that will be suitable, Inspector,' she said.

'Thank you, Miss Cole. Thank you.'

He took the box to the dining table and began to look through the photographs. They were mostly of Michele Pulman, who looked stunning in every one. Some were with her husband, and some with him and their daughter, but they were mostly of her. Many were studio photographs taken about forty years ago when she was eighteen or twenty, showing her wearing the flimsiest of costumes. The outfits were obviously stage clothes and made to titillate.

He looked round for Miss Cole but she wasn't there. It could have been because she knew the sort of photographs that most of them were. He had almost forgotten that he was looking for a suitable photograph of that two stone diamond ring. He put the studio photographs back in the box. Some of the later photographs of Mrs Pulman had her wearing the ring and eventually Angel found a suitable one. She was seated somewhere outside in a rose arbour or garden by herself. She had her hand up near her face and it showed the ring off to perfection. He took the photograph back into the drawing room.

When Angel returned to the drawing room, he saw that Michele Pulman's body had been collected and Mac had gone with it. The SOCOs were packing up their vacuuming and photographic equipment, tripods, spotlights and samples, mostly into white canvas bags and taking them out to their van. DS Taylor was wrapping the fingerprint block prior to packing it into a box. Miss Cole was standing at the foot of the bed, holding up her hand and wiping her black fingertips on a tissue.

Taylor came up to Angel and said, 'We've taken the bed and bedding to pieces, sir, but there's no sign of that ring.'

Angel nodded, then he turned to Miss Cole. He showed her the photograph and said, 'Right, Miss Cole. I have found this one. It's the one that best shows up the ring. Thank you.

When you're ready, I'd like a little chat with you about some of the other photographs.'

'Certainly, Inspector,' she said, then she looked at her black fingers and said, 'That's the best I can do until I get home and get some hot water and the pumice stone at them.'

'Let's go into the dining room,' he said.

They sat down at the table and Angel quickly found one of the more salacious photographs he had seen of Michele Pulman. He turned it over and read aloud the handwritten words, 'Michele Noble. Grounds for Divorce. May 1975.'

He added, 'I suppose "Noble" was her maiden name. But what does "Grounds for Divorce" mean?'

Miss Cole sighed. Then shook her head. 'That was the name of a group of dancers. Well, they called themselves dancers. They were all the rage in the seventies. There was this dreadful man . . . can't remember his name . . . oh yes, I can. It was Rupert Homer. Now Rupert Homer married a local dancer, Ernestine something or other . . . I forget . . . anyway, they formed a group of about sixteen girl dancers who used to perform outrageous and frankly, dirty routines. At first, I believe they started in clubs and pubs. He would play the piano and drive the van with the girls and their costumes — they were so flimsy — round the clubs in Batley, Manchester, Sheffield, Leeds and eventually on television. You must have seen them.'

Angel frowned. 'I don't think I did,' he said. 'If I had, from what you say, Miss Cole, I certainly wouldn't have forgotten. So Michele Noble, her maiden name, was a dancer with Rupert Homer's "Grounds for Divorce"?'

'Yes,' she said. 'She told me they also travelled abroad to Berlin, Paris and Rome. She said that Bromersley was geographically ideally suited for Yorkshire, Granada and the midland television studios.'

Angels eyebrows squished together. 'And what happened to Rupert Homer?'

'He must have died. He was about 50 in 1975, so if he was still living, he would be ninety now.'

'And what about Ernestine, his wife?'

'She'd be over eighty. I don't know, Inspector, but I expect she won't be around either.'

'Whereabouts did they hang out?'

'Ernestine started with a dancing school on Sheffield Road where Hammerton's auctioneers is now. I believe they lived over the shop, as they say. But as time went on they moved up here and lived somewhere on Creesford Road. I don't know exactly which number.'

Angel wrinkled his brow. 'Up *here?*' he said.

'Well, they could afford to, Inspector,' she said.

'Thank you, Miss Cole,' he said.

He rubbed his chin. He wondered why all the murders had taken place within ten minutes easy walking distance of each other. He was convinced that the murderer lived locally and didn't need any transport.

She looked at him, nodded and smiled as sweet as a pot of honey.

ELEVEN

It was five minutes past eight that Saturday night, when Cliff Grant closed the shop and locked the door. He had had a shave, was in his best suit and wearing a clean shirt, and with a small package under his arm, he set off along Canal Street in the direction of Wakefield Road.

There was very little traffic moving along the street, but there were a few cars parked outside the houses. It had been a hot day for May so that Saturday evening was pleasantly warm.

He was intent on seeing Maisie Spencer. Since that heated clash in the shop between her, Ann Fiske and himself, Maisie had been on his mind. Those big, flashing dark eyes and silver hair were not easy to forget, and pictures of her returned to him frequently, between cutting rashers of bacon on the antiquated bacon slicer, weighing out potatoes and washing pots in the kitchen sink. He didn't believe that Maisie meant half of what she had said to him when Ann Fiske was there. He reckoned given a chance he would be able to talk sense into her.

Ann would have been the more difficult of the two. She was more elusive and inhibited than Maisie. It was true that once the barriers were down, Ann was more responsive and passionate and their love-making almost always culminated in highly satisfactory mutual climaxes, but in other aspects of their relationship, she was challenging and wanted to dominate him.

However, Maisie was all woman and he reckoned that she was the one for him. She had always had a kind, gentle and forgiving nature. And he hoped she was in a forgiving mood that evening.

He passed 120 Canal Street and trusted that Ann Fiske had not been looking out of any of her front windows. He hoped also that her informant was otherwise engaged. He didn't want anybody in Ann's camp spreading any more stories about him.

A car was approaching from behind. The sound of the engine grew louder. He hoped it wasn't going to Ann's house. She could be a passenger and she was sure to recognize him. He resisted the temptation to look round. The car passed by. He glanced up to see if he knew the driver. He didn't. He sighed a little.

He strode out on Canal Street, increasing his speed until he arrived at number 24. He adjusted the package under his arm and knocked on the door. He ran a hand over his hair to flatten it down, pulled his tie tighter, and polished each of the caps of his shoes on the back of his trouser legs. Although unsure about how the meeting might work out, he was really looking forward to seeing her again. As he heard some movement at the other side of the door and the turn of a key, he put on his best Sunday smile.

The door was opened and Maisie Spencer of the big, sparkling dark eyes and even white teeth, looked out at him with a big smile and said, 'Yes?'

Then realizing who it was, she stopped smiling, pulled back her head and said, 'Oh. It's you. What do you want, Cliff Grant?'

'I want to see you, Maisie. I want to apologize and explain.'

'I thought I had made my feelings to you absolutely clear.'

'You did. You *both* did. Between you both, you got me very nicely over a barrel.'

'It took the two of us to show what a liar you had been.'

'I know, Maisie, but two against one isn't fair, is it? You and her tripped me up every time I opened my mouth. And what she said was not always the exact truth. It just looked bad for me. I didn't have a chance.'

Her eyes showed that she was wavering. He pressed the advantage.

'Come on, Maisie,' he said. 'We've known each other a long time now. We *had* been engaged for nearly ten months. We've always had a good time when we've been together, haven't we? I have always felt happier after being just alone with you, whether it was for five minutes or a few hours. I thought that you might have felt the same. I think in all fairness you should hear both sides of the case. Even a murderer is allowed that much.'

He noticed that her eyes were shining even brighter because they were moist.

She sniffed, but maintained the hard voice. 'You can come in for five minutes only,' she said, stepping back a little. 'That should be long enough for you to say what you've got to say. And I shall time you.'

'Thank you, Maisie,' he said quietly.

'Go into the living room and sit down,' she said as she closed the front door and turned the key.

Cliff went into the room. There was the usual clutter of women's magazines, *What's on TV* and newspapers on the chairs and the settee. The television was switched on with the sound off.

He went up to an easy chair. It had a stocking draped over the arm. He picked it up and looked round, wondering where to put it.

Maisie came in, saw him and her eyes flashed angrily. She quickly snatched it off him, rolled it up and put it in her pocket. 'I wasn't expecting anybody coming . . . not at this time,' she said.

Cliff sat down in the easy chair. He put the package on his lap.

Maisie picked up the remote control for the TV from the settee and turned the set off.

'You needn't turn it off for my sake, Maisie,' Cliff said.

'It's all right. It was a repeat, and I'd seen it anyway.'

He nodded and smiled.

She settled on the settee, pulling tight any creases in her skirt, then she straightened the collar of her blouse, put her hands on her lap and looked at him.

'Now then?' she said. 'What have you got to say? Make it quick.'

Cliff could see that she was not willing to make it easy for him.

He cleared his throat. 'First things first,' he said, and he passed the package that was on his knee across to her.

'What's this?' she said. She couldn't stop a small smile developing.

He smiled back and said, 'As if you didn't know. Open it. Go on. It's for you.'

She put her hand into an open end of the package and pulled out a red box with a ribbon across a corner. She peered at the writing on the top of the box. Her face lit up.

'Chocolate liqueurs,' she said. 'Oh, I didn't know. Thank you, Cliff.' She took off the lid and looked at the silver paper wrapping around each chocolate which was the shape of a miniature bottle. She saw some printing on the inside of the lid. 'Oh, and they're from Belgium, they look too good to eat.'

'Nothing's too good for you, Maisie,' he said. Then he added, 'And before you make any wisecracks, the box of chocolates I took to Ann Fiske was just an ordinary box of milk chocolates with different fillings.'

She looked across at him and beamed. After a few seconds her face hardened. She slowly put the lid on the box and said, 'Well they're certainly great, Cliff, and I do thank you for them. But I am not going to let you buy your way into my good books. You've played with my feelings for some time now and the time has come for us to have a proper understanding.'

Grant was thinking he had made some progress.

'Yes. Right, Maisie, maybe I have,' he said. 'Well, I am not going to try to paint myself as something special because I know I'm not. Nor will I ever be. But my life has lately been turned upside down. My mother gave me such a hard time that I had to leave home. I had to go. She was driving me mad. I got a job away from home and I was doing all right, but I was lonely. I missed you and I missed my home. So I eventually gave it all up. I came home. Next day, Ma's dead. Worse than that, she's been murdered. The police don't have a clue. I am now left living in that house by myself, living above the shop on my own. And I find it very hard. My mind is constantly on her. I'm . . . sort of . . . expecting her to appear and tell me what to do. Anyway I seem to have dropped into the business, and it seems a pity not to try to keep going, at least for the time being. But the place is so quiet some days, and absolutely silent in the evenings. Some nights when I have locked the shop door at eight o'clock, I think I'll go mad. So the other night, I got a box of chocolates and, seeking company and a change from the telly, I knocked on the door of Ann Fiske.'

Maisie's eyes flashed. 'I understand all that so far,' she said, 'but why did you pick on *her* first? After all, I'm the one you're supposed to be engaged to.'

'She's only a few doors from the shop,' he said. 'And I thought she would be more likely to be . . . erm available.'

'Available? What do you mean available?'

'Knowing how popular *you* are,' he said craftily, 'I naturally thought that one of *your* admirers would be courting *you*, whereas Ann Fiske would be . . . as I said, available.'

Maisie thought about this for a few moments. She liked the idea that Cliff thought she was likely to have a string of boyfriends battering her door down. *And,* specifically, in greater demand than Ann Fiske.

A slow smile developed across her face.

Grant noticed the smile and he thought he was doing well.

'Go on,' Maisie said.

'Well, there was a phone call,' he said. 'Her father had been rushed to hospital, so of course she had to go. And I came out, having only been there a few minutes.'

Maisie frowned. She pursed her lips, sniffed and said, 'A few minutes? . . . How long exactly is a few minutes?'

'A *few* minutes . . . five or ten, not more than ten. Don't you believe me?'

She looked at him with a knowing expression.

'Well, work it out, Maisie,' he said. 'I closed the shop at eight. Then I got washed, shaved, changed and walked to Ann's house. I was there only five or ten minutes. Then I left her house and legged it up here. I suppose I arrived at your house at about twenty past eight, didn't I?'

She nodded. 'I don't remember when you arrived exactly, but it couldn't have been much after that.'

He smiled. '*There* you are then,' he said. 'I was *lonely, desperate*. You know what loneliness is like. You told me how lonely you were after your little sister went to live with your mum and dad.'

It was true. Maisie did find the house bearing down on her most evenings, particularly since she was living on her own. She nodded and smiled. The smile lit up her face.

If Grant had had a flag and a flagpole, he would have run the flag up to the top. 'So are we still friends then, Maisie?'

'Of course we are,' she said, holding out her arms.

Grant leaped out of the chair to the settee opposite and they kissed very warmly. Then he broke away and said, 'There's something else, sweetheart.'

Her eyebrows shot up. She looked worried. 'What's the matter?'

'We are supposed to be engaged,' he said.

She frowned and nodded. 'Well, we are — only if you *want* to be.'

'Of course I want to be. What about you?'

'You know I do,' she said.

Then Cliff fumbled about in his jacket pocket, pulled out a small box, opened it and took something out. Then he reached out for her left hand, lifted her third finger and slid on a ring. 'Well, I want to seal it with this.'

Maisie was shocked. She snatched her hand back and gazed at the glittering clear stones and the white band on which they were set. 'Wow! Oh, Cliff. Are they real diamonds?'

He smiled. 'Of course they are *real* diamonds.'

'It's wonderful, Cliff. Absolutely wonderful. I've never owned a gold ring before. It *is* gold, isn't it?'

'It's platinum, actually. It's an antique platinum diamond ring.'

'These diamonds are huge. I thought you were going to get me a solitaire?'

'Well, I was, but this came along and I thought it was too good to miss. Do you like it?'

Her face lit up. 'Oh yes, Cliff. I think it's fabulous.'

She leaned across to him and gave him a gentle kiss on the lips.

He put his arms round her and held her very close.

'Oh, thank you, darling,' she whispered.

He licked his bottom lip. 'There is one thing, though,' he said.

She pulled her head back a little so that she could look him in the face.

'Might be a good idea not to wear it for a while, at least not out of the house.'

'Why?' she said joyfully. Then she waved an arm around, finishing with her hand pointing to the ceiling as she added, 'I want the whole world to know that we love each other.' Then her face changed. 'What's the matter? Are you ashamed of me or something?'

'Of course not. It's just that I don't want any repercussions from some of the people in the street. Particularly since my mother was murdered. And those other women. When all these inquiries are finished with and they've got the killer, it won't matter, will it?'

She frowned and stuck out her bottom lip. 'I'm not sure I understand, Cliff.'

'Well . . . erm, just do it for me, will you?'

'I can wear it when we're together in the house, can't I?'

'Yeah. Just make sure other people don't see it. That's all I'm asking.'

She wrinkled her nose then she looked fondly at the ring again. 'It's wonderful. And it's so unusual.'

He smiled.

'I've never seen a ring with two diamonds on it,' she said. 'Does it have any special significance?'

Angel arrived home on Saturday afternoon at six o'clock. He was not particularly pleased with life. A fourth body had been found and he was really no nearer to finding the murderer than he had been three murders back. Solving murders those days usually happened when the criminal made a mistake or when science came up with some irrefutable forensic evidence. At that moment, Angel had no knowledge that either had occurred.

Mary saw the mood he was in and tried to shake him out of it by playing a recording she had made of an old Doris Day and Rock Hudson film on the television, which he seemed to be pleased about. However, after about an hour, she looked across at his chair and found him fast asleep. She sighed and stopped the playback. She thought they could watch the remainder of it together the following day, Sunday, possibly at lunch time.

Sunday arrived and so did the newspapers, which Angel read eagerly until Mary pointed out that the lawn needed cutting before it rained. He had hoped she hadn't noticed, but that was only wishful thinking so far as Mary Angel was concerned.

As rain had been forecast for late in the afternoon and evening, Angel gave the lawn its first cut that year and managed to get the mower back in the shed just as the first spots of rain arrived. He then went into the sitting room, sat in his favourite chair, and looked out at the garden. He immediately began thinking about the murders . . . he was thinking that he had never before come across a female killer who was systematically murdering women according to a prepared list. If only he could reach into her mind and know what evil she was planning.

His thinking was interrupted by the ever-serene Mary, who came in carrying a tray of tea.

'*Songs of Praise* is starting in five minutes,' she said. 'Don't you want to see it?'

'Oh yes,' he said. 'Of course.'

He found the remote control and switched on the TV.

They usually enjoyed the programme even though it had drifted a long way from the great programme it used to be.

Mary sat down next to him and said, 'Dinner will be in about an hour.'

He reached out and put his hand on hers. She looked at him and smiled.

TWELVE

It was 8.28 on Monday morning, 11 May and Angel was in his office, having a quick glance through the mail. There were a couple of letters requiring prompt attention, which he would deal with, but there was nothing else requiring urgent attention, so he pushed it all to one side.

He picked up the phone and summoned Ahmed.

Ahmed came in. He didn't look happy, and, in a subdued voice, said, 'Good morning, sir.'

Angel looked up at him, frowned and said, 'Sit down, lad. Now what's the matter with you this morning?'

Ahmed didn't smile. 'Nothing, sir,' he said. 'Did you say you'd some jobs for me?'

Angel noticed that Ahmed had had his hair cut. 'Oh,' Angel said knowingly. 'You're still concerned about the fact that the Chief wants to see you on Thursday?'

'I'm very worried, sir. I can't think of what he could possibly want. You don't think that a member of the public has complained about me, do you? I've been trying to remember anything I might have got wrong or said wrong or something.'

'No. Not at all. It might be that a member of the public wants to *congratulate* you for something. Had you thought of that?'

He blinked and smiled briefly, then he reverted to wrinkling his nose and turning the corners of his mouth down. 'Oh, *no*, sir. I can't think of anybody wanting to do *that* either.'

'Well, you don't know. Look, I had to see him about something a few days ago. It was just something he wanted my views on, nothing very earth shattering. I have frequently been summoned to see him over the years. It is part of the job of being a policeman. The longer you have been a copper, the more times it will happen that he needs to see you. I must have been up there three hundred times in twenty years, and I'm still here. He won't bite. Now forget about it until Thursday. Sufficient unto the day is the evil thereof.'

Ahmed looked up. He smiled. 'That's from the Bible, isn't it?'

'The sermon on the mount,' Angel said, 'I think. Now can we get on? There's such a lot to do.'

'Yes, sir. Sorry. I feel a lot better now.' He had changed. He was his usual self. Smiling and alert.

'Good,' Angel said. 'I have some jobs for you.'

Ahmed took out his notebook. 'Right, sir,' he said.

Angel reached into his inside pocket and took out the photograph he had chosen from the box in the drawer at 13 Creesford Road.

'That's the late Michele Pulman,' he said. 'Do you see the two stone diamond ring she is wearing?'

'Yes, sir.'

'Can you get a decent sizeable picture of that so that it can be reproduced in a newspaper? I need it in about two hours.'

Ahmed blinked. 'I think so, sir. It may lose focus and want defining a bit by hand . . . I'll see what I can do.'

'Great stuff. Then I want you to go down town to the Barnes and Barnes office on Victoria Road, and collect a copy of Michele Pulman's last Will and Testament. It should be ready waiting for you. They are expecting someone from here to collect it. Then see what you can find out about the deaths of Dominic Pulman aged in his early to mid-fifties, and his and Michele Pulman's daughter, Annabelle, aged about twenty. I understand that they were in a road accident and died ten years ago. You might try the Births, Deaths and Marriages office, first.'

'Right, sir. Is that it?' he said, looking up from his notebook.

'Yes, Ahmed. As soon as you can,' Angel said.

Ahmed dashed out.

Angel then consulted his notes. There was so much to do. It was a question of priorities . . . which job to do next.

There was a knock on the door. It was DS Carter.

'Can I have a word, sir?'

'I'm a bit pushed, Flora. But come in, sit down, and keep it short. What is it?'

'I've been thinking, sir. The murders only seem to occur between five and eight in the morning, when the victim is on her own.'

Angel nodded. 'It had not escaped me, Flora.'

'Also, because the four victims were precisely sixty or just sixty-one years of age, isn't it likely that their deaths had something to do with school? I mean, when was *one* year more critical than when we were at school? It was used as a gauge to compare how clever we were, and that determined which class we were put in. Couldn't we find out which school each victim had belonged to? It might be that they all went to the same school and were all in the same class.'

'That's a very good point, Flora. And perfectly valid, but it is forty-five or fifty years ago, and we are fighting time. For all I know, there could be a fifth and a sixth victim before we found out which school the first four went to. But it's a perfectly valid idea. Look, grab hold of Ted Scrivens, and get him onto it. And you supervise him. Tell him that to be of any help at all, he will have to move very fast. All right?'

She smiled and her eyes shone. 'Right, sir,' she said.

She stood up to go.

Angel took out the brown envelope backs on which he made his notes and began to read through them. 'Just a minute. I've got another job for you.'

She sat down.

Angel then looked up from his notes and quickly briefed her about the salacious photographs found on Saturday afternoon at Michele Pulman's home and the story told to him by Miss Cole. Then he said, 'I want you to find out what happened to this Rupert Homer and his wife, Ernestine, and I want it quick. If they are dead, I want copies of their death certificates. If either is alive, I want their present address and ideally, their phone number. All right?'

'Right, sir,' Flora said.

'You have no idea how precious time is now, Flora. There are two women near here who are sixty or sixty-one years of age who may forfeit their lives any second. Nobody has come forward in response to our appeal, even though it was quite intensive. Bear that in mind as you make those inquiries.'

'I will, sir,' she said and she went out.

Angel watched the door close and then returned to his notes.

The phone rang. Angel picked it up. It was Don Taylor.

'On Friday, you asked me about the rice and the cauli-flowers, sir. You wondered if SOC has spent enough time looking at them. So I instructed a couple of men to have a considered look at the samples. Now, forensics has no standard schedules for comparing a food substance such as dried rice and fresh cauliflowers, so we have just used our eyes, our taste buds, and our common sense, and arrived at the conclusion that all four samples of foodstuffs recovered from each SOC are identical and have come from the same source.'

'There's no indication which shop or supermarket that they were presumably bought from?'

'No, sir. In addition, in the case of the cauliflowers, they were all bought, or harvested, we think, at the same time. In other words, a fresh cauliflower was not bought for each victim.'

Angel rubbed his chin. 'That means the killer bought six cauliflowers in one go. Or cut six cauliflowers out of his or her garden or allotment at the same time.'

'That's about it, sir,' Taylor said.

Angel rubbed his chin hard. He was wondering if there was anything he could do to take advantage of what SOC believed to be a fact, and that it would certainly be unusual for anybody to buy six cauliflowers at a time. Although supermarkets, shops, cafes, restaurants, schools, hostels and nursing homes might well do. In addition, there were all the allotment holders and keen gardeners who sometimes sell their excess produce, and they would never admit to taking payment for anything in case HMRC were secretly observing them. And there were a lot of allotment holders. To check on all those vendors of vegetables would be a colossal job. After some thought, he decided that there were too many outlets selling the item. There could be twenty more murders committed before they could complete the questioning and then the party they were seeking might have bypassed the screening.

'Right, Don. Thank you,' Angel said.

'There's something else, sir. Might be inconsequential. Did you know that Miss Cole was selling her house?'

Angel's eyes narrowed. He shook his head. 'No, Don,' he said. 'How do you know that?'

'I was out walking with my wife yesterday, and Lorna was curious to know which was Michele Pulman's house and which was Miss Cole's. So we came out of the park by the back gate and I pointed them out to her. I remembered the address of Miss Cole's was 6 Orchard Grove. We soon found Orchard Grove, which is a beautifully quiet side road. It was then that we saw the For Sale sign in the garden of number six. I found it interesting, sir. Might be nothing.'

'Are you and Lorna interested in buying it then?'

'Oh no, sir. It's out of our league. We could never afford *that.*'

Angel licked his bottom lip then said, 'Did you see who was selling it, Don?'

'Yes, sir. It was Watts and Wainwright on Church Street.'

'Thank you, Don,' Angel said. And he replaced the handset.

He was still mulling over what Taylor had said about the cauliflowers. He was still wondering if it really was possible to isolate the *one* person in or around Bromersley, who had bought six cauliflowers before the death of the first victim, Gladys Grant, on 5 May, when the phone rang. He reached out for it. It was Dr Mac.

'I said I would let you know if the wounds on the body of Michele Pulman were the same as the other three victims. Well, they are. And I can confirm that those wounds *were* the cause of death and that the dear lady died immediately.'

'Well, thank you, Mac. Did you discover anything different or unusual about the crime or the victim?'

'Michael, you know if I knew anything helpful, I would have told you straight out but I am sorry to say there was nothing.'

Angel wrinkled his nose. 'Right, Mac,' he said. 'Thank you. Goodbye—'

'Just a wee minute,' Mac said. 'You didna ask me what I caught on Filey Brigg.'

Angel sighed. 'Mac,' he said. 'I'm up to my eyes in it. But tell me. You'll tell me anyway.'

'I caught six mackerel. And I've sent a pair by my wife to your Mary as an apology for being so grumpy.'

Angel smiled. 'Well, that's very nice, Mac. Thank you. Thank you very much. Goodbye.'

He replaced the phone. It rang again before he had the chance to take his hand away. It *was* hot this morning! He snatched it up. It was DS Taylor.

'I think we've got something, sir,' he said. He sounded quite excited for a man who is normally placid and takes things as they come.

Angel blinked. His pulse went up twenty beats. He could do with a breakthrough. 'Yes, Don?' he said. 'What is it?'

'We took the waste bin as it stood from the kitchen at Michele Pulman's house, sir. And we've been going through it systematically, item by item. Near the top was an empty can of Monty's lager. We've checked it out and there are stacks of prints on it as clear as they come. They are not the deceased's, Michele Pulman's, nor Emily Cole's. In fact, from the size, they look like a man's. Anyway, I'll put the prints through our records and then through the national system and see if we come up with anyone.'

Angel smiled. 'Great stuff, Don. Let me know.'

'Oh yes, sir. I will. I *certainly* will.'

Angel dropped the phone back in its cradle and slowly rubbed the fingertips of one hand across his temple. One annoying and confusing point that occurred to him was that the witnesses' evidence to date had indicated that the murderer was a woman, yet Don Taylor, who certainly knew what he's talking about, said that the prints on the can appeared to be those of a man. That was something that Angel would have to reconcile.

He pulled out the old envelope he had in his inside pocket and looked down it for a telephone number. He picked up the phone again and tapped in the number.

Seconds later he was talking to Emily Cole.

'I was wondering if Mrs Pulman had had any visitors in the last few days of her life, Miss Cole?'

'No, Inspector, she didn't,' Miss Cole said. 'Last week, there was the community nurse who came on Monday, that was the 4th. And she was the only visitor all week apart from me.'

'Are you sure about that? It's very important.'

'I'm very sure, Inspector. Visitors could only see Mrs Pulman through me, you see, because I have her house keys.'

'Did you happen to stay in the room all the time the nurse was there?'

She hesitated. 'I think so,' she said. 'I usually do, in case Mrs Pulman wants my help answering a question or needs something. The nurse is a very nice, pleasant young lass who wouldn't harm a fly. She had been calling on Mrs Pulman for a few months.'

Angel licked his top lip. 'I expect she is, Miss Cole,' he said. 'I expect she is. Now I must ask you something else. Do you enjoy a drink now and again?'

Her reply wasn't immediate. 'I expect you mean an alcoholic drink, don't you?' she said. 'Well, I used to buy a bottle of sherry now and again to keep me warm in the winter, but to tell the truth, I can't afford it now.'

'So you don't drink alcohol at all then nowadays?'

'That is correct. And I don't really miss it.'

'What about Mrs Pulman? Was she partial to a drink now and then?'

'Oh no. Not at all. Anyway, she had some pills that helped her to sleep and the doctor instructed her not to take any alcohol with them as that would make her very ill. So she didn't. Going without didn't seem to bother Mrs Pulman, either.'

Angel pursed his lips. His pulse rate was increasing. His chest was warm and buzzing . . . it felt as busy as a beehive. 'Well, DS Taylor has found an empty lager can in the kitchen waste bin, have you any idea how it got there?'

Miss Cole was briefly silent. 'I can't explain *that*,' she said. 'I have no idea. I am the only one that puts anything in there. Mrs Pulman can't. It's well out of her reach. That's *very* strange.'

Angel's stomach rumbled. His chest quivered. Blood rushed to his face. That confirmed it. The empty tin can was the first whiff of a clue. The murderer had supped the Monty's lager, disposed of the empty can in the kitchen waste bin and had carelessly left his prints on it. Whoever's prints were on that can was the murderer of four women.

'Right,' he said, hardly able to conceal his excitement. 'Thank you, Miss Cole,' he said. 'Thank you.'

He slowly returned the phone to its cradle and as he withdrew his arm, he noticed that his hand was shaking. It was because he was near to a breakthrough in finding the murderer. It always affected him in that way. Also, he had the additional incentive that if he found the killer before his silver wedding anniversary on Thursday next, then only *three* days away, his friend Daniel Ashton, ex-cop turned antique dealer, had agreed to letting him have the solitaire ring for Mary for £500, thus saving £300 on his alternative price of £800. He simply *had* to solve the case by then because there was no way he could ever scrape together the £300 difference.

He returned to his notes. It was difficult for him to concentrate because he was desperately hoping to hear very soon that the fingerprints on the lager can that Don Taylor was searching for would turn out to be somebody they could quickly identify, charge and lock up, before they could murder anybody else.

There was a knock on the door. It was Ahmed. He was carrying two sheets of A4. 'I've got a couple of photographs of that ring, sir. I hope they are good enough. I've enlarged the photograph as far as it will go before it loses definition, and I've darkened some of the detail as it lost considerable contrast.'

Angel looked at them eagerly. He was favourably impressed. 'That's great, Ahmed. Leave them with me for now.'

Ahmed grinned. 'I'll get on with those other jobs, sir.'

'Right, lad,' Angel said and he reached out for the phone.

Ahmed went out and closed the door.

Angel tapped in a number. A voice said, 'Bromersley Chronicle, news desk.'

'Can I speak to the editor, Geoffrey Poole, please? This is Michael Angel, Bromersley Police.'

'Please hold.'

Several seconds later, the cheery voice of the editor came on the line.

'Yes, Michael. What can I do for you? Have you got a breakthrough in that serial killer case yet?'

'No, but we believe that our killer stole an unusual ring from his last victim and we have a photograph of that ring. If it has been seen by anyone since early last Saturday morning, we want to know about it.'

'And you want the Chronicle to give it some exposure, for free?'

'Yes, I do. Now Geoffrey, this case is ostensibly a local case. The victims are all local and I am pretty certain that the killer is local, so this appeal only needs to be local, which means I can offer it to the Bromersley Chronicle as an exclusive, without anybody accusing me or the force of partiality. Only afterwards, if it doesn't produce a positive result, then it might it be offered to other papers. All right?'

'Fair enough. We'll use the exclusive tag then and I'll give it front page exposure. We'll want that photograph in the next hour to get it in the next edition.'

'I'll get it to you promptly, Geoffrey, and thank you very much.'

'It's a pleasure, Michael, and thank you. Goodbye.'

Angel ended the call, and immediately tapped in a single digit.

A voice down the line said, 'Control room. DS Clifton.'

'Ah, Bernie. DI Angel. I want to get an envelope down to the Bromersley Chronicle office urgently. Will you get someone to collect it from me?'

'Right away, sir,' Clifton said.

Angel replaced the phone, opened a drawer in his desk, took out an A4 envelope and a sticky label marked "From Bromersley Police — URGENT". He slapped the label on the envelope, marked it "For the attention of the Editor, Geoffrey Poole Esq." Then he put the two touched up prints of the ring unfolded inside and sealed it. He had only just finished that when a PC in road patrolman's gear knocked on the door and collected the envelope.

He picked up the phone and tapped a single digit. It was soon answered.

'SOC, DS Taylor, can I help you?'

'Ah, Don, Angel here. How are you getting on with those prints?'

'Nothing positive yet, sir. The PNC has no record of them. We are going through the local and most recent prints we have logged, by hand.'

'Right, Don. Keep me posted,' he said. He hung up the phone and ran his hand through his hair. This waiting was wearing him down.

The phone rang. He reached out and snatched it up. 'Angel,' he said.

It was Detective Superintendent Harker.

'You're never off the bloody phone, are you?' Harker said. 'Don't you ever go out and interview your suspects face to face? Never mind answering that. You would only have come out with some annoyingly glib answer. Now, I want to see you, straightaway. I've got to go out in a few minutes and look at a bouncy castle to see if it's suitable for the Constabulary Mid-Summer Party, so I can only spare you five minutes.'

Harker ended the call.

Angel bared his teeth he was so angry. He slammed down the phone. Jumped up from his desk, pulled open the office door and made his way up the green painted corridor. By the time he'd reached Harker's office door, much of the paddy had left him. He knew he would gain nothing from saying anything he would regret, but there were limits to his patience.

He knocked on the door and went in.

The office, as usual, had the atmosphere of an orchid hothouse and the smell of an old-fashioned chemist's.

The little man was at his desk. He looked up. 'Come in. Sit down.'

Angel chose the seat directly opposite the superintendent where he could see him between the tall piles of books, ledgers and papers.

Harker picked up a sheet of paper, glanced at it and said, 'Did you make two overseas calls to two different numbers in Ontario, Canada on a telephone in this station last Saturday at 10.31 and again at 10.36?'

Angel had to think back. That was the day Michele Pulman was murdered. 'Yes, sir, on the phone in my office,' Angel said. 'Why?'

Harker's face hardened. 'But that was Saturday,' he said. 'You don't work Saturdays.'

'I worked *last* Saturday because — with my team — I was called out to a triple nine on Creesford Road, the serial killer's fourth victim, Mrs Michele Pulman. It was a long day.'

'Well, that explains why you were in your office on Saturday, but it doesn't explain why you phoned Canada.'

Angel sighed. 'I phoned Canada to trace the next of kin of the dead woman, sir.'

'And did you find him or her?'

'Yes, sir. It was a cousin . . . a woman.'

Harker sniffed. 'And is the cousin coming over the ocean to identify the body?'

'Oh, no, sir.'

Harker went scarlet. 'Oh, no, sir. Oh, no, sir,' he said, attempting to mimic Angel. 'Well, what was the point of the exercise then?' he bawled. 'Why didn't you send an email to the Ontario Provincial Police? That would have cost nothing.'

'A phone call gives you more flexibility, the opportunity to sense the nature of the person you are talking to and the ability to detect their attitude to their dead relative.'

Harker's fists clenched and unclenched. 'We're not dealing with attitudes and senses. We're dealing with *facts*. Was he at the scene or *wasn't* he? Did he have a weapon or *didn't* he? Are his prints on the weapon or *aren't* they? Did he have a motive or *didn't* he? And so on. We're not into attitudes and senses. They'll not count a penny in court. I don't know how you ever became a policeman — especially a detective. Are you any nearer solving this cauliflower serial killer business or not?'

'We are, sir. We have a lager can from a waste bin at Michele Pulman's home, which is plastered with a man's prints. Yet no man lives there or has been in the house recently to the housekeeper's knowledge. If we can find the owner of the prints, we will have the serial killer.'

'Oh. My goodness, look at the time,' Harker said. He stood up. 'You'll have to go, Angel. Or else I shall be late.

Well, I don't know what to do about these phone charges. I can't pass £28.00 for two telephone calls to Canada. You'll have to watch these stupid, unnecessary charges, Angel. Well, go. Go. Get out of it, man. You're making me late. Some of these fairground amusement people are very wealthy and don't like to be kept waiting.'

Angel came out of Harker's sweatbox, stormed down the corridor to his own office.

A few moments later there was a knock at Angel's door.

Angel rubbed his face all over with a hand as if to obliterate the memory of the last few minutes with Harker, then he said, 'Come in.'

It was DS Carter.

'Oh, it's you, Flora.'

She could tell he was not his usual self.

'Are you all right, sir?'

'I will be in a minute,' he said. 'What is it?'

'I've found Ernestine Homer. She's in a retirement home on Sheffield Road. She's eighty-six but, according to the manageress, has all her wits about her.'

Angel's face brightened. 'Great stuff, Flora,' he said rubbing his chin. 'I must see her. What's the address?'

THIRTEEN

It was eleven o'clock exactly when Angel was shown into the small bedsit room of Mrs Ernestine Homer at the Belmont Ladies Retirement Home, Sheffield Road in Bromersley. She was propped up with pillows in a comfortable looking upholstered chair near the window, so that she could see what was happening outside.

'Do come in and sit down, Inspector,' she said.

Angel moved a dining chair nearer to her. 'Thank you, Mrs Homer.'

'It's to do with the dancing school and my dancing ensemble, "Grounds for Divorce", isn't it?' she said.

'Yes, it is. Do you mind if I put this little recorder here to save time writing out notes?'

'Not at all, Inspector. This is quite a new experience for me, being interviewed by the police, especially at my age. I hope you won't be battering me with a truncheon,' she said with a little titter.

He smiled at her and said, 'I'll try and restrain myself, Mrs Homer. Now, I have it right, don't I? In the 1970s, one of your pupils was Michele Noble, who later married and changed her name to Pulman?'

She nodded. Her double chin wobbled. 'That's quite correct,' she said with a smile. 'A most beautiful and charming girl.'

'Tragically, Mrs Homer, I am investigating her murder.'

Her bottom lip trembled. 'Murder?' she said. 'Oh dear. I hadn't heard.'

'I'm sorry to have to bring you the news. Now, can you tell me anything about her?'

'Well, it's such a long time ago . . . Michele Noble . . . she was excellent, very likeable young girl, very popular with the boys I believe, as were all of our young ladies for that matter.'

'Can you remember anything in particular about her?'

'No. You tend to remember those who *were* trouble. There's really nothing more I can say about her.'

'How many pupils did you have, Mrs Homer?'

'Hundreds and hundreds over the years. Mothers used to bring their little dears from as young as five. Mostly girls but a few boys. Initially, I had to try to teach them rudimentary things like dancing in time with the music. It was not always easy. I had classes of all ages sub-divided according to their ability. Some children made it, but a lot didn't. And when they reached twelve or thirteen many of them lost interest.'

'This was before you started "Grounds for Divorce", I suppose.'

'Well, I kept the school going as well. The school was our bread and butter. After all, we had to keep supplying and replacing the girls who weren't suitable for GFD. Those who hadn't the looks, the ability, were unreliable or ill, or put on weight.'

'Do you have any registers or lists or group photographs that would enable us to trace any of them?'

She held out her hands, open and facing upwards, and said, 'Rupert kept the books and had stacks of photographs and publicity stills. That stuff all went to the tip when I gave up my home to come here.'

'Would you remember any of the other three women who have also been murdered?'

Mrs Homer put both of her shaking hands up to her mouth. 'Oh dear. I didn't know there were any more.'

'Sorry to have shocked you, Mrs Homer. And, of course, they may not have been pupils of yours.'

'Oh dear,' she said, her hands still shaking.

Angel then read out the maiden names of the other three murdered women one at a time, and showed recent photographs of each one. Mrs Homer thought she remembered them all and believed that they had been dancers in 'Grounds for Divorce' but she could not be at all certain. And she was unable to tell him anything specific about them.

'If they *had* all been dancers in "Grounds for Divorce", Mrs Homer, can you remember any others so that we can protect them?'

'I'm very sorry, Inspector,' she said. 'My memory is not what it was. You are asking me to go back over forty years!'

Angel sighed. It was clear that she could be of no help to the investigation. He thanked her for her help, took his leave and raced back to his office at the police station.

The phone rang. Angel reached out for it. It was Taylor. There was excitement in his voice. 'The prints on the can of lager belong to Cliff Grant, sir.'

Angel's eyebrows shot up. His mouth dropped open. 'Cliff Grant? There's no possibility of a mistake, Don?'

'Absolutely not, sir. There's his thumb and three fingers and a palm print, all Grant's. Also, there are no other person's prints on it.'

'Right, Don. Great stuff. I'll get a warrant immediately and I will want your team to give the house and shop a thorough search. Take the house to pieces brick by brick, if necessary. Stand by.'

'Right, sir.'

Angel returned the phone to its cradle, jumped up from behind his desk, went out of his office across the hall to the CID room. He pushed open the door. The only detective there was Crisp. He was at his desk looking at a computer screen and tapping away into it. He looked up and saw Angel. He called across. 'Looking for me, sir?'

'Yes, but I am also looking for Ahmed.'

'He's out, sir. I think he said you'd sent him to find out about the death of Michele Pulman's husband and their daughter.'

Angel recalled that he had sent him to Births, Deaths and Marriages.

'Of course,' he said. 'And where's Flora?'

'Don't know, sir. She was around a few minutes ago.'

'Hm. Come on through to my office.'

As they went out of CID together, they bumped into DS Carter.

'I want you, Flora. I want both of you in my office now.'

When Angel's office door was closed and the three of them were settled, Angel told them about Cliff Grant. They were both surprised.

Angel said, 'So we need to work fast. First of all, we need a warrant to bring him in for questioning and another to search the house and shop.' He looked at Crisp and said, 'Will you get those, Trevor?'

Crisp nodded and stood up to go.

'I should apply to Mrs Flood,' Angel said. 'She's a JP, she's the nearest and she'll most likely be at home now. Hurry up.'

'Right, sir,' he said and he dashed out.

Angel picked up the phone, turned to Flora and said, 'I know you've a lot of inquiries in hand. Pop off, but don't go far. You never know when you might be needed.'

'Right, sir,' she said, and went out.

He tapped out a number on the phone. The call was to his opposite number in the uniformed division, Inspector Asquith.

'Michael Angel here, Haydn. Can you let me have three of your lads to bring in a suspect who may be armed with a knife?'

'Is this chap the serial killer, Michael?'

'Yes, I am pleased to say he is. Just got the evidence against him. I am waiting for a warrant. Will you have your men come to my office in about ten minutes?'

'To pick that man up will be a pleasure. They'll be with you before then.'

'Thank you, Haydn.'

Ten minutes later, at 1.20 p.m., three police vehicles left quietly from the car park at the rear of the police station. Firstly, armed with the two warrants, was DS Carter and Angel in his car, then next were three uniformed police constables in the patrol car, which was followed by DS Taylor and his team in the white SOC van.

As Angel turned right out of the car park, Flora said, 'I realize that we have proof that Grant had the *opportunity* to be in Michele Pulman's house, sir, but have we also got proof that he had means and motive as well?'

'We've got him for all three, Flora. It was well-known that he and his mother didn't hit it off. He disappeared off the face of the earth for eight months just to get out of her way. However, from what I understand, he hadn't the ability to live independently without her. He tried to make it work. It obviously didn't. So he came back. They presumably had a row, he saw how easy and simple his life could be without her, so he took a knife to her. That's motive. Well, for means, it was simply a common domestic steak knife out of the kitchen drawer, and opportunity, well, he lived there and he was there. He could choose his own time. What more do you want?'

'I can see all that, sir,' Flora said. 'But that only explains the murder of Gladys Grant, sir. What about the other victims?'

'I've been thinking for some time that the killer wanted only *one* of the victims dead. The others were to hide the significance of that death, thereby obscuring his motive. It sets we "stupid" coppers scurrying round trying to discover what relationship these dead women have to one another, when there isn't any.'

'I see what you mean, sir. But what about the cauliflower and the rice? What are they all about?'

'I don't know. Maybe Grant will tell us that,' Angel said as he turned left onto Canal Street. He checked in his mirror that the two vehicles behind him were still there.

They travelled in silence to the end of that long street. Angel turned left at the end onto Sebastopol Terrace and stopped outside the shop.

The three uniformed were first out of their patrol car. One went round to the back door. The other two went in by the shop door followed by Angel and Carter. The bell rang loudly over their heads. There were no customers in the shop. One of the constables turned the sign on the door round to show it was closed. Then the two constables made their way through the gap in the counter to the back when Grant came through from the kitchen. He was smiling but the smile left him when he saw the grim faces of the two uniformed police at his side of the counter. One of them moved very close to him, the other went through the kitchen to the back door and let the third policeman in. They came into the shop and moved up to Grant, whose eyes slid rapidly from side to side, taking in the new and entirely unexpected situation.

'What do you want?' Grant said.

The older of the uniformed constables said, 'Have you got anything sharp on you, sir? In your pockets or . . .'

'No,' he snapped. 'Of course I haven't anything sharp. What is this?'

'Would you empty your pockets out onto the counter, sir?'

Grant's face went scarlet. 'No,' he said. 'I won't.'

Angel said, 'You should know, Mr Grant, that I have a warrant here to arrest you for questioning in connection with the murder of your mother, and three others. I also have another warrant to search this house and shop. Now you can cooperate with us and come quietly, or you can protest and be difficult, but the end result will be the same.'

Grant looked slowly at the grim faces of Angel, then Carter and then at the PCs. He made a snorting noise and said, 'I do it under protest, I tell you. I'm not guilty of harming my mother or anybody else for that matter. It's an outrageous accusation.' He then felt in the pockets of the blue overall and took out a tissue and a bunch of keys and tossed them on the counter. Then he unfastened the buttons down the front of the overall so that he could reach his trouser pockets. He emptied them ending with a big wedge of paper money from his hip pocket. 'There,' he said.

'Is that everything?' Angel said.

'Yes,' Grant said.

Angel said, 'Now put your hands in the air while the constable searches you.'

'*No*! I don't *have* to do this,' Grant said. 'I haven't done anything wrong.'

'If you haven't anything to hide, you wouldn't mind being searched, would you? It's only the guilty who would have any objection.'

Grant glared at him and slowly put up his hands. The constable patted him down.

'Turn round,' the constable said.

Grant slowly obeyed. The constable made quick work of the patting down his back then said, 'Lower your hands and face the front.'

Grant slowly turned.

The constable looked back at Angel; his expression indicated that everything was satisfactory.

Angel said, 'Now, put your hands behind your back, wrists together.'

'This is bloody outrageous! I want to see a solicitor.'

'We'll organize that as soon as we get to the station, Mr Grant,' Angel said.

The corners of Grant's mouth were turned down. 'You'd better,' he said.

'You can depend on it, Grant,' Angel said. 'It is the law of the land. We *have* to do it. Now put your hands behind your back. The handcuffs will come off at the station.'

With his head down, Grant diffidently put his hands behind his back.

There was the quick click and rasp of the handcuffs and everybody except Grant relaxed.

Angel looked at the uniformed policemen and with a jerk of the head instructed them to head back to the station.

By holding his arms, the policemen manoeuvred Grant out of the shop and into the car. Don Taylor and the SOCO team came in then.

Angel looked at Flora and pointed to the contents of Grant's pockets on the shop counter. 'Take charge of that lot. Put it in an evidence bag and bring it along.'

Angel then turned to Taylor and said, 'You know what we want, Don. All the usual things, plus anything to do with Monty's lager, cauliflowers, dried rice, a two stone diamond ring, a long sheepskin coat and photographs or any reference at all to an elderly woman with grey hair. All right?'

Taylor scribbled them down in his notebook. 'Right, sir,' he said.

'And make sure all your team know,' Angel said. 'Phone me, if you find anything.'

'Right, sir.'

'We're off,' Angel said. Then he turned to Flora and said, 'Are you ready?'

FOURTEEN

Angel was in his office, checking over his notes.

Flora knocked on the door and came in.

Angel looked up at the clock. It was exactly two o'clock.

'Is Mr Bloomberg still with Grant?'

'Yes, sir. They're in interview room number one, ready and waiting.'

Angel looked up. 'Oh. Right, Flora,' he said.

He picked up his notes and pen, put them in his pocket and made his way to the door.

'Did we have any denims that fitted Grant then, Flora?'

'Oh yes, sir. He looks all right, but he doesn't like them of course.'

'Never known a suspect that did. Have his clothes been carefully bagged and sent down to SOC?'

'I took them there myself, sir.'

Angel nodded. 'Good.'

They went out of his office into the corridor.

A PC was stood in front of the door of interview room number one, which was conveniently next door. The PC could see Angel's intention so he moved to the side and opened the door for him.

'Thank you,' Angel said, and he and Flora went inside and closed the door.

Bloomberg, a short, bald-headed man in a dark suit was seated next to Grant at the table. Grant was dressed in army fatigues. He now seemed bright-eyed and confident.

'Ah, Mr Bloomberg,' Angel said. 'I understand that you have completed your discussions with Mr Grant.'

'Yes, Inspector. We are ready.'

'This is DS Carter,' Angel said. 'She'll be sitting in with us.'

Bloomberg nodded and Flora Carter smiled politely at him.

Angel reached over to the recording machine, checked that there was a new tape in it and pressed the red button. It lit up and the spools in the cassette recorder began to rotate. He then made the necessary opening, stating the date, time and place and giving the name of all four people present.

Then Angel looked at the young man and said, 'Mr Grant, do you enjoy a drink from time to time?'

Grant looked at Bloomberg, who nodded.

'Yes. Of course,' Grant said.

'Would it be correct to say that you prefer lager to whiskey?'

Grant frowned. 'Yes. I suppose so.'

'Do you have a favourite brand of lager?'

'Well, I suppose I would enjoy any of the most well-known brands, why?'

Angel rubbed his chin. 'Well if you had *choice* of any UK brewed lager, which would it be?'

Grant's forehead creased. He looked at Bloomberg who nodded.

'Well,' Grant said, 'out of any I would choose Monty's lager. Why?'

Flora looked at Angel. He noticed out of his eye corner but didn't react.

'*Monty's*,' Angel said forcefully. 'Well, Mr Grant, would it surprise you to know that an empty can of Monty's lager was found in the waste bin in the kitchen of the house where Michele Pulman was murdered? It was discovered shortly after her death, and it has your fingerprints all over it.'

Grant took a deep breath, pulled his head back, frowned and said, 'Frankly, Inspector, it amazes me. I don't think I know Mrs Pulman or where she lives and I've certainly never been in or near her house. There must be some mistake.'

'There's no mistake, Mr Grant. Fingerprints do not lie.'

Grant looked desperately at Bloomberg.

The little man looked at Angel and said, 'Inspector, do you have any other evidence — *however unlikely* — to put before Mr Grant?'

Angel's eyes flashed. 'I have no more evidence at this time, but I assure you that *that* evidence is not at all unlikely, Mr Bloomberg,' he said. 'I have witnesses who will swear to where and when the lager can was found, and to confirm that Mr Grant's fingerprints are all over it.'

Bloomberg said, 'My client has duly noted that, Inspector, and will answer it in due course. So, do you have any other evidence to put before him?'

Angel said, 'Not at this time, but I have more questions I would like to put to him.'

Bloomberg whispered something into Grant's ear, who pulled a face then nodded.

Angel looked down at his notes. He knew exactly what he was going to say but it gave him several seconds to cool down. The interview was being recorded and he had to try not to lose his temper or show any lack of control.

He looked across the table and said, 'Mr Grant, where were you between 5 a.m. and 8 a.m. on Saturday last, 9 May?'

'At home, in my own bed until around 7.30. Then I got up. I have to have the shop open by 8.'

Angel pursed his lips. 'Erm . . . Was anybody else in the house or the shop with you who can confirm that you were there during that time?'

Grant glared at him and said, 'Of course not.'

'Oh, dear me,' Angel said. 'That's very awkward. That's the time that Mrs Pulman was stabbed and died.'

Grant said, 'Erm. Yes, I am very sorry to hear that, but it has nothing to do with me.'

'And what about between five a.m. and eight a.m. on the mornings of 6 May and 7 May?'

Grant's face went red. 'The same. I was at home on my own.'

'Did anybody see you through the window, during either of those times, do you remember? Or did the phone ring? Did you speak to anyone on the landline?'

Grant shook his head. 'I was asleep. I always sleep until the alarm clock wakes me up at 7.30.'

'That's very awkward, Mr Grant,' he said. 'You see, those are the times that two other women were murdered.'

Grant raised his shoulders, opened his hands in front of him and said, 'What's awkward about it? I had nothing to do with them.'

'We'll see,' Angel said, rubbing the lower part of his face with his hand.

Bloomberg said, 'Excuse me, Inspector. Is there anything else you want to ask my client?'

Angel's face creased. He licked his bottom lip with the tip of his tongue. Then he looked at Flora who shook her head.

'No,' Angel said. 'Not at this time.'

It was 8.28 on Tuesday morning, 12 May, when Angel arrived at his office. It was only two days away from Mary's and his twenty-fifth wedding anniversary. He was feeling pleased with himself for obvious reasons, but not least because Daniel Ashton would *have* to let him have the £800 solitaire ring for £500 because he had caught the serial killer *before* their anniversary. Those were the terms of the deal he had with him. There wasn't much time.

The phone began to ring. It sent all thoughts of wedding anniversaries and solitaire rings straight out of the window.

He reached out for it.

It was a young PC on reception. 'Sorry to disturb you, sir, but there's a young lady here called Maisie Spencer, who is asking to see you. She says it's in connection with the arrest of Cliff Grant.'

Angel frowned. He rubbed his chin. Of course, he would *have* to see her. It could very well be more valuable evidence.

'Bring her down to my office, Constable,' Angel said.

'Right, sir,' the PC said.

It was at that moment that Angel realized he hadn't seen Ahmed since he had sent him to do some jobs in the morning of the previous day, and that was before Don Taylor had found out that the prints on the lager can belonged to Cliff Grant. Angel was particularly concerned about him because of the conversations they had had regarding his appointment to see the Chief Constable on Thursday morning. Angel hoped that he hadn't done anything stupid.

There was a knock on the door. 'Come in,' Angel called.

It was the PC with the young woman. 'Detective Inspector Angel, miss,' he said.

Angel stood up.

She looked at him and then brought her hands up to her mouth. She glanced round the room. She didn't seem to like what she saw.

'This is Miss Maisie Spencer, sir,' the PC said.

'Thank you, Constable,' Angel said as he looked at the curvy, silver blonde as she came in.

The constable touched his forehead, went out and closed the door.

She stood by the door. Her hands were round her mouth. One hand held a tissue. Her hair was all over the place and there were dark brown streams of eyeliner running down her cheeks. Her soft appealing eyes looked over her hands at Angel, who smiled benevolently back at her.

'Come in, Miss Spencer. Please sit down,' he said.

She took a small step forward, then in a small voice said, 'Maisie.'

He smiled. 'Maisie,' he said.

She nodded and took the seat directly opposite him.

'What can I do for you, Maisie?' he said, resuming his seat behind the desk.

She wiped her eyes and said, 'I'm sorry . . . I am such a mess, Inspector.'

Angel shook his head. 'That's fine,' he said.

She took in a deep breath and said, 'I was told that you have arrested Cliff Grant because you think that he is the serial mur . . . mur . . . murderer. Well, I know for a fact that he couldn't be.'

'Tell me about it, Maisie.'

'Well, last Friday night, I spent the whole night with him. He's perhaps too nice to tell you that, Inspector. He couldn't be in two places at the same time. That woman, Mrs Pulman. I don't know what time she was mur . . . mur . . . it happened, but it couldn't have been Cliff. He isn't like that. Anyway, I was with him. And the previous Tuesday and Wednesday nights, when those other women . . . when it happened to them, it couldn't have been Cliff because I was with him, all night.'

Angel looked at her. He rubbed his chin then said, 'Do you sleep around a lot, then, Maisie?'

Her face muscles tightened. 'That's not sleeping around,' she said. 'We're engaged to be married.'

Angel instantly looked at the back of her left hand, and saw a two stone diamond ring on her third finger. His eyes shone and his eyebrows shot up momentarily. His heart began to beat like a loud drum. He couldn't take his eyes off it.

'When were you planning to get married?' he said.

'Soon, but we hadn't talked about a specific date.'

'Hmmm. How long have you been engaged then, Maisie?'

'Some time now, Inspector. Almost a year.'

'Is that ring your engagement ring?'

She relaxed a little. She smiled and pushed her hand forward closer for him to see. 'They're not cubic zirconia. They're *real* diamonds.'

He looked at the ring. It matched exactly the description of Michele Pulman's missing ring. He rubbed his chin.

She looked at his face. She was disappointed that he didn't seem to like the ring. 'Don't you think it's fabulous?'

'It is. It is. It's beautiful. Have you had it long?'

'Cliff gave it to me four days ago. Saturday night.'

Angel's fingers rubbed his forehead really hard. Michele Pulman was murdered early that same day. What *was* he going to say to this young woman?

'Well, where did *he* get it from?' he said.

'Dunno. I didn't ask him. The two stones represent him and me. My mother reckons that those two stones will add up to more than a carat.'

Angel nodded. He had an idea. He took out his notes from the inside pocket of his coat and looked down it for a phone number.

Maisie Spencer looked at him and frowned.

'Excuse me, just a minute, Maisie,' he said. 'There's something I have just remembered I must do.'

He picked up the phone and tapped in the number.

Maisie looked round the room. It wasn't really what she thought a detective's office would look like.

The phone was soon answered.

'DI Angel, Bromersley Police, is that Miss Cole?'

'Oh, yes, it is, Inspector,' she said. 'What can I do for you?'

'Something has come up, Miss Cole. I wondered if you could come down to the station.'

'Do you mean *now*?'

'Yes. If you could. I can organize transport if that is a problem?'

'Well, yes, I suppose so. I'd certainly appreciate that. Very well. I can be ready in five minutes, Inspector.'

'I'll send a car for you then, straightaway.'

Angel cancelled the outside call then tapped in a digit for the control room and made the necessary arrangements to transport Miss Cole from her home to his office.

He replaced the phone and turned back to Maisie Spencer.

'Excuse me, I had to do that,' he said.

'That's all right, Inspector.'

The phone rang.

He looked at it and said, 'I'll *have* to answer it. I'm sorry about this.'

'That's all right, Inspector. I'm in no hurry.'

It was DS Taylor of SOC. 'What is it, Don?'

'We're back from searching Grant's shop and house, sir,' Taylor said.

'What did you find?'

'We found twenty-four cans of the same lager, Monty's, in exactly the same size and pattern cans as the one found in Michele Pulman's house.'

Angel nodded. He was thinking that that was good ammunition for the prosecution. 'Anything else?'

'Yes, sir,' Taylor said. 'Our team here in the station have vacuumed Grant's shop overall and extracted several grains and dust of dried rice from the right-hand pocket. I've checked them against the rice used in the course of murdering the four women and it matches.'

'It matches? No doubt about it?'

'None, sir.'

He ended the call, replaced the phone and looked at the bewitching face of Maisie Spencer. He rubbed his chin. 'Maisie,' he said. 'I have asked a lady to come in to have a look at your engagement ring. I hope you don't mind.'

Maisie smiled. 'I don't care who sees it,' she said. 'It's the most fabulous ring, isn't it?'

'Do you mind waiting for her?'

'No. Not at all. I told you, Inspector, I'm in no hurry.'

'Good,' Angel said and reached out for the phone. He dialled a single digit.

A female voice answered, 'CID.'

'Is Detective Constable Ahaz there?'

'No, sir. This is DS Carter. Can I help?'

'Oh, Flora, yes, you can . . . but where's Ahmed?'

'Didn't you send him to a solicitor's to collect a Will and then to Births, Deaths and Marriages about something?'

'I did, but that seems a long time ago. I hope he's all right.'

'I could see if I can follow him up, sir.'

'Well, yes, Flora, perhaps later. There's something I want doing now. Come across to my office, will you?'

He ended the call and moments later DS Carter came in.

Angel introduced the two young women to each other. Then he said, 'Maisie, would you mind waiting in the interview room next door for a few minutes? DS Carter will get you a cup of tea and stay with you while you wait. There are some urgent matters I have to see to. Won't keep you long.'

Maisie got up. 'Not at all, Inspector.'

They went out.

Angel then went down to the cells and found the duty jailer. 'Is Grant all right? Are there any problems?'

'He's fine, sir. No problems at all.'

'Good. Let me in. I want to talk to him a while.'

The jailer unhooked a key from a board and went across to a cell with "Grant, Cliff. DOB. 28.6.85" written in white chalk on the door.

Angel followed him.

The jailer opened the trap window in the door and saw the prisoner laid out on his bunk, reading a very much thumbed newspaper. Then the jailer put the key in the lock and opened the door.

'Lock me inside,' Angel said.

Grant put the paper down, sat up, swivelled round and put his feet on the floor.

'Everything all right, Grant?' Angel said.

'What have I done to have the great and almighty Inspector Angel visiting me?'

Angel stood at the foot of the bunk and looked squarely at the man. Grant looked washed, smart enough but he needed a shave.

'I've had your fiancée, Maisie, here. She says she was with you last Friday night. By the way this chat is off the record. I am not wired up with any recording device, nor is anyone listening. I am hoping you will make my life simple and tell me the truth.'

'I have always told you the truth, Inspector, and look where it's got me.'

'Maisie said she was with you at the shop last Friday night last, Tuesday night and Wednesday night and stayed until around eight o'clock the following morning. If it's true, of course, it gives you a powerful alibi, if it's false and we discover that it is false, it will make you look like a conniving monster.'

Grant sighed and ran his hand through his hair.

'There's more,' Angel said.

He proceeded to tell him about the finding of rice in his clothes. Grant's jaw dropped.

'I have no idea how *that* could have happened, Inspector. We don't even have dried rice in the shop.'

Angel then said, 'Miss Spencer also showed me the two stone engagement ring you had bought her. Where did you get it from?'

The muscles in Grant's face tightened. He seemed surprised that Angel knew anything about it. He looked down. 'I bought it privately,' he said.

'Who from?'

Grant's eyes travelled to the left and then to the right, then back again. 'A man. I don't know who it was.'

Angel didn't believe him. 'And how much did you pay for it?' he said.

'Forty pounds.'

'*Forty pounds*?'

'He wanted fifty, but I beat him down.'

Angel thought it must have been the bargain of a lifetime.

'I can't say anything more about it, Inspector. I really can't.'

Angel reckoned that Grant couldn't say anything more about it because it was a lie. Grant had come by it, by simply taking the ring off Michele Pulman's finger after he had murdered her.

He looked Grant slowly up and down. The policeman felt that he was looking at the murderer of four blameless women, including one of them being his own mother. He had stabbed her with an ordinary domestic steak knife after a row. Then, as he would have been the obvious number one suspect, he went on to murder another three women of similar age in exactly the same way to confuse the investigators. Then to mystify them even further, he had introduced rice, cauliflowers and four short verses of bad poetry.

Angel left Grant and returned to his office.

FIFTEEN

Angel returned to his office to find Miss Cole sitting quietly and tidily facing his desk and DS Crisp leaning against the wall.

When Angel entered, Crisp came away from the wall and said, 'I took the liberty of showing Miss Cole into your office, sir, because I knew that you would be in a hurry to see her.'

'Thank you, Trevor,' Angel said as he passed in front of him to get to his desk. 'You've done well.' Then he looked across at Miss Cole. 'Are you comfortable there, Miss Cole? Is there anything you would like? A cup of tea or—'

'Nothing, thank you,' she said.

Angel reached his swivel chair and sat down. 'Sorry you had to wait,' he said. 'We won't waste any more of your time.'

He stood up and said something quietly into Crisp's ear. Crisp nodded and went outside. A couple of minutes later, Maisie Spencer came in, followed by Carter and Crisp. The latter closed the door. Maisie saw Emily Cole sitting, knees close together, back straight, facing Angel's desk. She frowned then forced a smile and nodded towards her. Miss Cole nodded back politely.

Angel said, 'Do you two ladies know each other?'

Both Maisie and Emily shook their heads.

Angel looked quickly at them both and seeing no recognition in either's face, he introduced them.

Then he said, 'I have brought you two ladies together, so that Miss Cole can see your beautiful ring, Maisie. Will you show it to her?'

Maisie was delighted, and held out her left hand for Miss Cole to see.

When Miss Cole saw the ring, she jumped out of her seat, rushed over to her, raised up her arms and in a loud voice said, 'Oh my god! Oh my god! How did you come by it?'

Maisie frowned. 'My fiancé gave it to me. It's very unusual, isn't it?'

'Can I have a closer look at it, please?' Emily Cole said.

Maisie pressed her lips into a fine line. Her eyes narrowed. She looked from Miss Cole to Angel then back. After a moment, she slowly slipped the ring off and passed it to the old lady.

Miss Cole snatched it off her, turned away, held it up to her eyes and peered inside the ring shank, then tried to put it on her little finger. The ring was too small for her puffed up and ancient fingers. She gave the face of it another thorough examination then turned to Angel and said, 'Yes. This is *the* ring, Inspector. No doubt about it.'

Maisie, open-mouthed, stared hard at Miss Cole.

Angel held out his hand. Miss Cole reached over and put the ring into it. As soon as it touched his hand, Angel was reminded of his wedding anniversary in two days' time and his need to get a move on if he was going to secure that solitaire.

Maisie said, 'What does she mean, Inspector? "This is *the* ring. No doubt about it"?'

Angel turned to her and said, 'Evidence has been given that this ring was stolen by being removed from the body at the time of the murder of Mrs Michele Pulman, Maisie.

So that means I'll have to take possession of it for the time being.'

Maisie said, 'But that's not right, Inspector. Cliff gave me that ring. He wouldn't take it off a dead woman and give it to me. It's not right. He bought it, fair and square. He wouldn't be party to any murder. I shouldn't have my ring taken off me like this. Cliff is innocent of these murders.'

Angel looked at her and said, 'Miss Spencer, if it is proven that the ring has been bought fair and square and was not stolen then, of course, you will certainly be entitled to have it returned to you. But I wouldn't hold out much hope.'

Maisie's eyes welled with tears.

From her corner seat, Miss Cole said: 'I wouldn't hold out *any* hope at all, Miss Spencer. That ring by rights belongs in Mrs Pulman's estate.'

Maisie glared at the old lady. Then she turned back to Angel.

'Oh, Inspector, this can't be right. Nobody has ever given me a ring before.' She covered her face with her hands. 'Oh, can I see him?' she added.

Angel said, 'No, I'm sorry, Maisie.'

'We *are* engaged,' she said.

'It's not possible yet, Maisie. I'm sorry.'

'But he's innocent, I'm sure of it.'

There was a knock at the door.

'Come in,' Angel said. It was Ahmed.

Angel's face lit up. He looked up and down the young man. 'Are you all right, Ahmed? Where have you been? I haven't seen you since yesterday morning. Just a minute.' He turned to the two women and said, 'Thank you both for coming in.'

They both looked at their feet. Neither seemed to have anything else to say.

He rang reception, asking for a police constable to escort the two ladies to the waiting area near the front door of the station, then he rang the control room and organized transport for them.

When the constable arrived at Angel's door to collect the two women, Maisie burst into tears. Angel hated to see her so upset. He patted her gently on the back, but he could not find any words to comfort her. Miss Cole looked very solemn as she followed the constable and Maisie up the corridor.

Angel closed the door thoughtfully. He returned to his chair behind the desk.

'Right, Ahmed. Sit down and tell me what you've been doing,' Angel said. 'Those two jobs didn't take you a full working day, did they?'

'Well, collecting the Will from Barnes and Barnes was easy enough, sir,' he said, putting a long brown envelope on the desk in front of him.

'Ah good, thank you. What took you so long with checking up on Mrs Pulman's late husband and late daughter?'

'Well, sir, neither of the deaths were recorded in the Bromersley register. Nor the Barnsley register, nor the Leeds register—'

Angel frowned. 'Have you been to the Bromersley, Barnsley *and* Leeds register offices?'

'Yes, sir. I finally found them in the Huddersfield register office. Then I went to the local newspaper offices where I eventually came across a pretty comprehensive report on the accident.'

'And how did you get to those places?'

'By bus and train, sir. There are quite decent services to those towns from here.'

Angel smiled. 'You shouldn't have gone to all that trouble without ringing me back. At the time, it was important. Now it's less so.'

Angel brought him up to date with the arrest of Cliff Grant and an outline of the confirmatory evidence that had subsequently rolled in. He finished by saying, 'As you've invested so much time and legwork in it, you might as well tell me quickly what you found out.'

'Right, sir,' Ahmed said taking out his notebook. 'Well, one evening in January 2005, Dominic Pulman was taking his daughter, Annabelle, back to university on the country road. There had been a heavy fall of snow that day, and at a particularly treacherous corner, the car skidded. It went off the road, down a gully, through the ice at the bottom and into a body of water two metres deep. They were found two days later.'

Angel pulled a grim face. 'Sounds dreadful. You'd better write up your notes — even if it is only to justify your expenses.'

'Right, sir,' Ahmed said, then he ran his fingertips across his chin a few moments. 'There is one thing I'd like to ask about the arrest of Cliff Grant, sir.' Angel looked at him and nodded. 'Well, I thought that you were thinking that the killer was female, sir. I wondered what had changed your mind. That's all.'

Angel rubbed an eyebrow with his fingertips. 'It's like this, Ahmed,' he said. 'Science is never wrong, is it?'

Ahmed frowned. He looked at Angel. He wondered if he was asking a trick question.

Angel sniffed and in a louder voice said, 'Well, Ahmed, is science ever wrong?'

'Scientific tests, conducted in laboratory conditions can't be wrong, sir, I suppose, but deductions based on the results of those tests can be wrongly interpreted.'

'That's exactly the point. The graphologist said that the writer of the verses was a man, middle-aged, and emotionally unstable.'

'And do you agree with that, sir?'

'Well, it shows that he knows his job.'

'So we are definitely going with male, are we, sir?'

'We have to, Ahmed. We *are* logical people, aren't we? I have enough evidence to put Grant away for a very long time, whether it is in a prison or a secure hospital.'

Ahmed shrugged slightly and held his open hands palm side upwards. 'But that doesn't explain the grey-haired woman, sir.'

Angel's nose turned upward and he said, 'No, I know it doesn't. Look, Ahmed, you'd better go and write up your notes. I don't want you telling me that I have probably got everything wrong. I can do that for myself.'

Ahmed grinned. 'Right, sir,' he said.

He went out and closed the door.

Angel ran his hand through his hair. He sighed, then he looked across his desk to see what he must do next. There was no time to lose. If Grant was *not* the murderer, then the lives of two other women were still at risk. Then he saw the long brown envelope that Ahmed had brought in from Barnes and Barnes. He reached out for it. It wasn't sealed. He shook out the contents. It contained several large sheets of paper fastened together at the corner with a piece of pink tape. He straightened the papers out and saw the heading, "The Last Will and Testament of Michele Gloria Pulman".

Angel read it quickly. It was really very simple and it had only been made six months ago. Everything was bequeathed to Emily Cole provided that she was still in the employ of Mrs Pulman at the time of her death.

Angel rubbed his chin. The words of Gerard Barnes, her solicitor came back to him. Barnes had said, 'Mrs Pulman was a very wealthy woman.'

He put the document down, pushed the swivel chair away from the desk, tipped it back as far as it would go and stared up at the top of the office wall and the ceiling. He closed his eyes and tried to think clearly. This was proving to be probably the most difficult case he'd ever taken on. He was still a thousand miles away from knowing what a cauli-flower, a throat and mouth filled with rice, and an elderly woman with grey hair had to do with . . .

Then he had a brainwave.

He opened his eyes, sat forward in the chair, pulled open a drawer, took out a copy of the local telephone directory, and whizzed down the Ws until he came to the entry for 'Watts & Wainwright, Church St, Chrtd Survyrs'.

Ten minutes later, Angel was in the offices of Watts & Wainwright.

'Mr Wainwright? I'm Inspector Angel. Thank you for seeing me promptly. Is there somewhere we can go where we can talk privately?'

'Yes, of course, in my office,' Wainwright said, leading him through. 'It's through here, Inspector. This is it. Please sit down.'

'Thank you,' Angel said.

'My receptionist said you were interested in 6 Orchard Grove, Inspector,' Wainwright said. 'How may I help you?'

'Yes. I understand that the owner, Miss Emily Cole, is selling it?' Angel said.

'It *is* for sale, Inspector, but it is not owned by Miss Cole. She is the tenant.'

Angel's eyes narrowed. He pursed his lips. 'Where is she moving to?' he said.

'I don't know. She will have made her plans, I suppose. She was given six months' notice to quit on 1 December of last year. So she will be out by 1 June.'

'I don't suppose she will be looking forward to moving at her age?'

'She doesn't. Recently she asked for an extension beyond the 1 June. We have put it to the vendors, Hawker Properties PLC, and they are considering it, but frankly, I don't hold out much hope.'

'What was she hopeful of achieving by extending the notice period?'

'Well, erm . . . Can I speak to you in confidence, Inspector?'

'We *are* speaking in confidence, I hope, Mr Wainwright. It applies both ways.'

'Of course. Of course. Well, she *said* that she could possibly raise the capital for an outright purchase if she was given a little more time.'

Angel rubbed his chin. That was significant news.

Wainwright said, 'But as she had been having considerable difficulty keeping up with the monthly rent, the vendors do not consider her as a serious prospective cash purchaser of the property. Besides, there are several other parties interested in the property, so I expect to conclude a sale quite soon.'

'I understand,' Angel said.

He took his leave of Wainwright and drove straightaway to 6 Orchard Grove. It was easy to find because of the For Sale sign protruding out at the front.

From the outside, Angel thought it was a very fine-looking small, detached house, which had been built in the thirties, and was located up a short, quiet road in the affluent district of Bromersley. He parked the car at the side of the road, walked up the garden path through the long, immaculately maintained weed-free borders to the front door and pressed the bell push. He heard the bell ring out in the house. He waited. But there was no reply. He tried again and waited.

Next door, he heard a car engine. Then it stopped. There was the slam of a car door. Shortly after that, a man's voice called through a thick privet hedge.

'Hello there. Can I help you? Are you looking for Miss Cole?'

Angel looked toward the privet in the direction of the voice and said, 'Yes, sir. Where are you? I can't see you.'

'Can you come to Miss Cole's front gate?'

'Yes, of course,' Angel said, then he made his way along the garden path back towards his car. He reached the gate, opened it and saw the man next door standing with a hand on his drive gate. He gave Angel a big smile.

'Just been out to do a bit of shopping,' he said. 'Lucky I saw you. You would have been standing there all day. I saw her leave early this morning in a taxi. She had two big suitcases. Looks like she's gone away for a holiday.'

Angel frowned, introduced himself then said, 'Do you happen to know where she was going?'

'No idea,' he said. 'I called out to her as she was locking her front door, and she pretended not to have heard me, but I know she isn't deaf. She seemed eager to get away and was not prepared to be delayed with friendly chit chat. She's a strange old woman. My wife and I have tried to be good neighbours, heaven knows.'

Angel thanked him. He got in the BMW, made a three point turn out of Orchard Grove and when he reached the main road, he reckoned cogs were falling into place. In the first two murders, an old woman with grey hair in a sheepskin coat, who "might not be the full shilling," was spotted leaving the crime scene. That could easily have been Cole. If he could find the sheepskin coat in her house or in her possession, it would be sufficient to arrest her. Also, she could have easily planted an empty Monty's lager can into Mrs Pulman's waste bin. And Cole was also in the best possible position to have been able to steal the two stone diamond ring which, contrary to what she had said, Mrs Pulman may have removed from her finger years ago, dumped in a drawer and forgotten about.

Suddenly, things were looking grim for Emily Cole.

When he arrived at the police station, Angel went straight to the duty jailer to be admitted into Grant's cell.

Grant looked up from his bunk. 'Back again, Inspector? What do you want *this* time?'

Angel's jaw muscles tightened. 'You ought to be damned grateful to me, Grant. I'm trying to get you off these charges but you're not helping me and you're not helping yourself.'

Grant frowned. 'Well, all right, Inspector. What do you want from me?'

'Primarily, I want the truth,' Angel said.

'I've always told you the truth,' Grant said.

'Have you?' Angel said, staring at him.

'Yes, I have,' Grant said, staring back. Then he added, '*I have*, but while we're on about that, Inspector, I hope you will realize that my girlfriend, Maisie, was only trying to give me an alibi. She wasn't with me those nights she told you about. And I hope you aren't going to be rough on her for trying to help me.'

Angel softened. 'Thank you for that, Grant,' he said. 'However, I never did believe her. I'm not malicious. I'll just strike it out and pretend she never said anything of the sort.'

Grant sighed. 'Thank you.'

Angel rubbed his chin thoughtfully. 'You know, I don't think you realize what sort of a mess you're in,' he said.

Grant frowned. 'Huh? It couldn't be much worse. Charged with murder. Stuck here in a cage . . . What do you mean?'

'Well, hasn't it occurred to you that somebody is deliberately trying to pin these murders on you?'

Grant's mouth dropped open. He stared at Angel.

Angel could see he had made an impression. 'Can you think of anybody who might dislike you sufficiently to set you up like this?' he said.

Grant shook his head several times and looked down. 'No,' he said. 'How awful. I know I'm not whiter than white, but I've never done anybody any *real* harm in my life. I have maybe led some girls on . . . but they've led me on as well. It's not *all* been one-sided. No. I can't think of anybody, Inspector.'

'Well, that's something you should think about,' he said. 'If any name comes to you, let me know. Now, let's quickly take the evidence against you. You have to tell me how you came by that two stone diamond ring.'

'I told you, I can't give you a name. I gave my word.'

Angel hesitated. 'Well, that's something else you should think about. Let's move on.'

After a few moments, he said, 'Now, there's the matter of finding rice in the right-hand pocket of your shop coat.'

'I've no idea how that got in there, Inspector.'

'Well, it must have been deliberately planted there. There is only a pinch of the stuff. But the murderer would have had to have been pretty close to you. I mean, if anybody had to lean over to reach your pocket, you would have been suspicious, wouldn't you? Who has been really close to you?'

Grant's bronzed face creased, then he said, 'Well, I suppose Maisie and Ann. Can't think of anybody else.'

Angel said, 'Maisie Spencer I know, who is this Ann?'

'Ann Fiske. She *was* a girlfriend of mine. Teaches music.'

'Have Maisie or Ann any bitterness towards you? I mean, can you see either of them wanting to exact their revenge on you?'

Grant hesitated. Then he said, 'Well, not Maisie, Inspector. Certainly not.'

Angel sniffed. 'What about this Ann Fiske?'

'Well, I dunno. We used to be very close, but I haven't been in touch with her for about a week.'

Angel exhaled and shook his head. 'A week. And she's not tried to visit you here, has she? A woman in love might think a week is a hell of a long time, Cliff,' he said. 'I've found that women can be very vindictive in certain situations. You'd better give me her address. I'll check her out.'

Grant rattled off the address. '120 Canal Street, Inspector, but I don't think Ann would be *so* spiteful.'

'Maybe not,' Angel said, scribbling down on his envelope. 'Leave it with me.'

Grant nodded.

Then Angel said, 'Then, there's the presence of two dozen cans of Monty's lager — your favourite — on the shop premises. Well, it only supports your penchant for the stuff, nothing more. By itself, it proves nothing. However, the finding of the can in Mrs Pulman's waste bin is damning. And your fingerprints are all over it. They are *not* faked. They are definitely *your* prints. Can you recall an occasion when someone gave you a can of Monty's lager and you handled it with both hands and then returned it?'

Grant shook his head slowly. 'I've certainly supped my share, Inspector, over the years . . . usually direct from the can, but I cannot remember an instance when I handed a can — full or empty — back to anybody.'

'They wouldn't have actually taken the can from you in their hands. If they had done that, they would have left *their* dabs on it. It would be somebody telling you to put the can down there or on that shelf or—' Angel broke off. His face suddenly brightened. 'I was going to say — or drop it in that bag. As a matter of fact, I saw that actually happen. A week today, last Tuesday. Yes. In the early evening. I remember I was sat in the car outside Cheapo's store in their car park. I was waiting for my wife. It was a dreadful day. The rain was beating down and the powerful wind was whisking it in every direction. The sky was black. It made it almost as dark as night. An old lady came along and dropped a can of Monty's lager and it rolled away from her, and a tall young man without a hat or umbrella, saw it, ran after it in an almighty downpour, stopped it rolling away, picked it up and—'

Grant suddenly said, 'It was *me*!' His eyes shone. His face brightened. 'I remember it exactly. It was early Tuesday evening. And it *was* a can of Monty's lager. It *was* a grey-haired old lady . . . and now I think about it when I returned it to her, she just held an open shopping bag out towards me and I dropped the can in there, and she *never did touch it*.'

'That's right,' Angel said. 'I saw it happen. So it was *you*. Can you describe the old lady?'

Grant shook his head. 'Just a grey-haired old lady.' His eyes opened wider as he ran the scene back through his memory again. 'Come to think of it, I remember she did look odd. She didn't want me to see her face. I didn't think anything of it at the time.'

'Did she *say* anything?'

'Only a squeaky thank you — nothing else.'

Angel rubbed his chin and with half-closed eyes said, 'A squeaky thank you. Pity. Well, anyway, *that* explains the prints on the can.'

Grant sighed and then smiled.

Angel then said, 'That woman could very well be our murderer. I don't suppose you noticed the car number plate, or the make of the car?'

'I didn't think about the number, but it was a red Polo. A newish one.'

Angel blinked then stared at him. 'Are you sure?'

'Yes. A red Polo. Late last year or early this year.'

Angel's heartbeat began to race. 'That's terrific. So it would have the number of the year, 14 or 15 among the letters on its number plate, wouldn't it?'

'I suppose so. Yes.'

'Do you remember anything else?'

'No,' Grant said. 'Only the scratches and the small dent in the bodywork just under the rear licence plate. She probably backed into something like a pipe sticking up out of the ground or the corner of something. I remember cos I thought what a pity it was for it to happen to a new car.'

Angel's heart missed a beat. He had solved crimes with less evidence than that.

'Well, Grant, that let's take you off the hook. I am happy to dismiss the murder charges against you, but there's still the one of withholding evidence regarding how you came to be in possession of the stolen two stone diamond ring.'

'Oh, Inspector, I didn't know it was stolen. And you wouldn't want me to break my promise to the person who sold it to me, would you?'

Angel shrugged. 'Well, if you won't, you won't.'

'I can't. I gave that person my word.'

Angel pursed his lips. His eyes creased. 'Well, I'll have to leave you locked up then. I should ask the officer to arrange for your solicitor, Mr Bloomberg, to come here and see you. And do tell Bloomberg about the dropped charges and the outstanding one.'

Grant smiled. He sighed. 'Wow!'

Angel called the jailer and asked him to let him out of the cell. He let Angel out then locked the cell door.

Grant stood up. He watched him leave, ran a hand through his thick, black hair and then sat down again. He was relieved to be off the murder charges, but he was still locked up.

Angel went straight up to the control room and up to the duty officer's desk. He was pleased to see it was an old buddy of his in the chair, Sergeant Clifton.

'Ah, Bernie,' Angel said. 'I've got an urgent message I want transmitted to all personnel in this station, and I want you to include the traffic wardens.'

'Right, sir,' Clifton said and he passed him a notepad and ballpoint pen. 'Would you like to write it down?'

Angel wrote: Urgent. Be on lookout for almost new red Polo saloon car wanted in connection with recent murders of four elderly women. It has a small dent and several scratches at the rear of the car under the number plate in the middle of the panel. Do not apprehend driver, who is extremely dangerous, but record registration number, phone in and keep under surveillance at a discreet distance.

He passed the pad over to Clifton. He quickly read it and said, 'It'll be texted right away, and I'll pass it on to the duty sergeant on the afternoon shift.'

Angel nodded. 'Thanks, Bernie. And if there's a sighting, let me know on my mobile.'

'Sure thing,' Clifton said. 'Sounds promising, sir.'

Angel felt a quiver of excitement in his stomach. He hoped that someone spotted the car soon, before another woman was murdered, and checked his mobile to make sure it was switched on.

He came out of the control room and went to his own office, knowing where he had to go next. He phoned for Ahmed then reached out for his raincoat.

Ahmed knocked and came in with a big smile on his face. 'I've just got your text, sir,' he said. 'Does that mean you've got a new lead?'

Angel's eyes sparkled. 'I hope so,' he said. 'I'm going to see a woman called Ann Fiske. I am not expecting to be gone long. If you need me, ring me on my mobile. All right?'

SIXTEEN

It was 12.20, when Angel drove the car into Canal Street. He allowed the BMW to run over the uneven cobbles at its own speed, right up to the door of number 120.

There was a little girl on the pavement, playing with a ball on the wall of the house next door. When she saw Angel, she grabbed the ball and ran through the ginnel nearby to the back door.

Angel locked the car and went up to the front door of number 120 and banged on the knocker.

Out of his eye corner he saw the imitation lace curtains of the house next door move slightly. He banged the knocker again. There was still no reply. Then from the house next door, he heard door bolts being shot back, followed by the turning of a key. He heard the door open and saw the head and shoulders of a woman with teeth as big as a racehorse peer round the door jamb. She was in curlers under a voile headscarf and wearing a pink house coat.

'Miss Fiske is out,' she said. 'What do you want?'

'What time will she be back?' Angel said.

'She's a purry-pathetic teacher, you know. And she moves from school to school. She *might* be back for her dinner hour. Depends where she's at. Where you from? You can leave a message with me, if you like.'

'If she comes home for lunch, what time would she be here?'

'What time is it now?'

Angel looked at his watch. 'It's 12.25.'

The woman pulled a face, making her look even more like a Derby winner. 'Oh well, you've missed her,' she said. 'She won't come now. If she'd been coming, she'd have been here by this time.'

'Thank you,' Angel said. It was annoying. He wasn't at all pleased. He really did need to speak to Miss Fiske.

A car suddenly arrived at the door of number 120. A man with grey hair was driving it and there was a woman seated next to him.

Angel looked up.

The woman from next door said, 'Oh. Look. She's here now. Oh, she's got a lift from Mr Prendergast. He teaches mathew-matics and algie-baba at the central school, you know.'

Ann Fiske got out of the car, looked up at Angel, frowned, turned back to the car driver, thanked him, closed the door and he drove away.

The neighbour said, 'This gentleman wants to see you, Ann. He's been waiting for you. I don't know who he is, but er . . .'

Ann Fiske gave her a sweet smile and said, 'Right, Gloria, thank you.' Then she turned to Angel. 'What can I do for you?'

Angel smiled at her and took his ID out of his inside pocket and showed it to her.

Her eyebrows went up.

'Shouldn't take long, miss,' Angel said.

She nodded and said, 'Right, come inside.' She put her key in the front door and turned it. 'Follow me,' she said.

'Is everything all right, Ann?' the neighbour said from the pavement.

'Yes, thank you, Gloria,' Ann Fiske called. Then she closed the front door with a bang.

'Please go through, Inspector Angel. Sit down. I haven't much time. I have to be at St Thomas's School on York Street at 1.55. What can I do for you?'

'I am investigating the deaths of several local women, and have a man, Cliff Grant — I believe you know him — charged with the murders.'

From the movement of Ann Fiske's eyes, Angel could see that she was absolutely astonished and that her mind was busy assimilating what he had said and how she should respond.

'Well, excuse me, Inspector,' she said, 'but that's ridiculous. I know or perhaps I had better say, *knew* Cliff Grant very well indeed. He is a rogue where women are concerned. He's lazy, shiftless, sometimes sly, but there is no hatred in him at all. I don't believe he could even kill a spider.'

'As you knew him so well, can you tell me what his relationship with his mother was like?'

'Well, awful. Truly awful. She was tempestuous, ill-tempered, domineering . . . they didn't get along. But despite that, there was also a powerful mother-son relationship. He would run away. He already had done, last year, rather than stand up to her. If you are thinking that Cliff could kill anybody — even his tyrant of a mother — frankly, that's ridiculous.'

Angel nodded. 'But there is a lot of evidence against him. And I wonder if you can help me with this? Some traces of dried rice, the same as that found at the scene of each of the murders, was found in a pocket of the blue smock coat he usually wore in the shop. He says he doesn't know how it got there, but, when pressed, he listed the people he had been really close to who could have slipped the rice — only a pinch of the stuff — into his pocket. You were on that list.'

Her eyes opened wide. 'Are you asking me if I put a pinch of dried rice into his smock pocket?'

'Yes,' Angel said, 'exactly that.'

'Of course I didn't,' she said. 'I wouldn't do anything to harm him. I loved Cliff, Inspector. Until recently, I was madly in love with the handsome great lump. I really thought that I could straighten him out, tidy him up, find him a job that suited his personality, and that we could have lived happily ever after. But I realized that he wouldn't have changed sufficiently for me to be happy, and I would only have made his life a misery. So I decided that he was not for me, even though since his mother died he has changed considerably. He's taken on the shop and from what I can see he is running it sensibly, conscientiously and enjoying it. The responsibility is suiting him. Anyway, Inspector, I have now given up all ambition I may have had in his direction. He has his eyes set on Maisie Spencer and I wish them both well together. I certainly wouldn't do anything to harm him.'

Angel pursed his lips. He had expected her to be possessive and bitchy and vindictive, but she was all sweetness and light. He was confused. He couldn't understand her. Ah well, he thought, she *was* a woman! And that he shouldn't always expect to comprehend their logic. He stood up to go.

'Well, that's all I wanted,' he said. 'Thank you very much, Miss Fiske.'

Angel arrived back at his office at 3 p.m. He took his mobile out of his pocket and placed it on his desk. He looked at it from time to time. He was very anxious for it to ring. Around 130 policemen and women, including the traffic wardens, were out there in the streets and in car parks, mingling among the public, checking on every red Polo car they might see. If it was there, one of them should spot it.

There was a knock at the door. 'Come in.'

It was Bloomberg. 'Can I have a brief word, Inspector?'

'Of course you can, Mr Bloomberg. Sit down a minute.' Angel indicated the chair opposite his desk. 'Grant will have told you about the murder charges being dropped.'

'I'm very pleased to hear it. However, there is the matter of the possession of a diamond ring. Of course, Inspector, you will know that you can't hold him for that. You will *have* to release him and then charge him for that separately, to be heard later.'

Angel licked his bottom lip with the tip of his tongue. 'I know, Mr Bloomberg,' he said. 'I know. I wonder if you can work with me on this?'

Bloomberg frowned. That didn't seem likely.

'Confidentially,' Angel said. 'The murderer of the four women has been trying to frame Grant for the murders, and as long as Grant is — or appears to be — locked up, the killer won't strike again.'

Bloomberg's face creased. 'I see what you mean.'

'Whereas if Grant was released and returned home,' Angel said, 'the killer would know that the plan has failed, and would almost certainly resume the murders.'

'You can't be sure of that, Inspector.'

'It's more than likely, though.'

Bloomberg wasn't happy. 'Well, my client would *have* to know that you no longer believe him to be guilty of the murders,' he said. 'I would *have* to tell him that. And I must say that I must advise him *not* to accept your proposal. It would be on his record for years and be possibly wrongly interpreted by a court in the future. He has a business to run and the longer he is away from it, the more it will deteriorate. I must remind you it is his only source of income.'

The corners of Angel's mouth turned down. 'Yeah, I understand that,' he said, then he rubbed his chin. 'Well, I hope that you will nevertheless put it to him. And there's something else.'

Bloomberg raised his eyebrows. 'Oh?'

'He refuses to say how he came into possession of that diamond ring, which, according to the victim's carer, has been stolen. That charge will still stand.'

'I can't comment on that, Inspector.'

'No. Of course you can't. I just wondered if you thought he would now be willing to make a statement about how he came by it.'

Bloomberg showed no emotion. 'I'll put it to him.'

The phone rang.

'Excuse me,' Angel said as he reached out for it.

It was a young PC at the reception desk. 'Sorry to bother you, sir, but there's an old lady here who is asking to see you. Her name is Miss Cole.'

Angel's jaw dropped. His face creased. 'Is she short, grey-haired and speaks nicely?'

'That'd be her, sir.'

Angel couldn't believe it. The sensation of a forest fire began to rage in his chest. His pulse was racing. 'Don't let her out of your sight. Keep your eye on her. Imagine that she's Lord Lucan. I'll be up right away.'

He replaced the phone, turned back to the solicitor and said, 'You must excuse me, Mr Bloomberg. Something very important has come up. You'll put those points to Grant?' He made for the door.

Bloomberg stood up. 'That's all right, Inspector. Yes, I'll go back to Grant, discuss those points with him and let you know what he decides.'

Angel looked back briefly and called, 'That's fine.'

Bloomberg followed him out of the office and closed the door.

Angel rushed up the corridor towards reception. He opened the security door with his ID card and looked around. Unusually, there was nobody sitting in the waiting area. He peered through the little inquiry window into the reception office and saw a couple of young PCs gawping at computer screens and tittering.

'Hey, you lads,' he said. 'I'm looking for a Miss Cole.'

'PC Hardy is with her in the interview room, sir,' one of the young PCs said.

Angel whipped round and pushed his way through the door into the interview room. There he saw the diminutive figure of Miss Cole with her handbag on her lap seated opposite the door, looking uncomfortable. A PC was facing her, standing with his back to it.

Angel sighed with relief and said, '*There* you are, Miss Cole. Thank you, Constable. I'll look after Miss Cole now.'

The PC went out. Angel pushed the door to.

Emily Cole was all of a twitter. 'Oh, Inspector. My nosey next-door neighbour said that you had called at my house this morning. I thought it might be something important.'

Angel glanced down at the black handbag on her lap. He had never noticed her handbag before. He thought that it could easily have held a knife. He would be very careful.

'Well, yes, Miss Cole. As a matter of fact it is very important. I noticed the For Sale sign outside your house. I thought you had said you liked the neighbourhood.'

'Oh, I do. I do,' she said. 'But you see, the house isn't mine. The owner wants to sell it and consequently I have to move.'

'Oh dear,' Angel said. 'And where are you intending on moving to?'

She slumped in the chair. 'That's the rub, Inspector,' she said. 'I haven't much of a choice. I may have to live with my sister and her husband in Warrington, or take — if I can get one — a warden supervised flat, either here or in Warrington. My brother-in-law is exploring the possibility of buying the house and renting it back to me at a rent I could afford. He's quite well off and may see his way to being able to do that, but he says the property is far too expensive, so he's talking to the agents. I am not optimistic. I went to Warrington this morning to take a few of my treasures in preparation for the evacuation on 1 June. It's all very upsetting.'

'I'm sure it is, Miss Cole,' Angel said. He was thinking that her explanation sounded reasonable enough, and there were some parts of it he could actually check on. Also, it really seemed as if she still didn't know that she had inherited Mrs Pulman's substantial estate.

Angel took out his brown envelope from his inside pocket. 'What is your brother-in-law's name, Miss Cole?' he said.

'Oates, Nigel, and my sister's name is Adele.'

He scribbled them down on the envelope and put it back in his pocket. 'Good. Well, that's that,' he said getting to his feet. 'Thank you for coming in.'

Her eyebrows shot up. 'Is that all you wanted to know, Inspector?'

'Yes, thank you. For now,' he said.

'I always feel much better after I have met you, Inspector. You always make me feel normal when so many people, especially young people, seem to think that old people are stupid and just so much of a nuisance.'

Angel grinned at her and opened the room door. 'Goodbye, Miss Cole.'

'Goodbye, Inspector,' she said and she toddled off towards the revolving door.

Angel turned away. He stuck his card in the internal security door and went down the corridor back to his office.

He was met at the door by Bloomberg.

'You want me?' Angel said. 'Come in. Sit down.'

'No need,' Bloomberg said. 'As predicted, Inspector, my client wants to be released immediately, and he has no comment to make about a diamond ring. He and I understand that the charge for his possession of it still stands.'

Angel wasn't pleased, but Grant was well within his rights. 'Very well,' he said, running his hand through his hair. 'I'll sign a release order for him straightaway. He can be out of here in a few minutes.'

'I'll go and tell him,' Bloomberg said. He rushed off.

Angel went into his office, completed and signed a release order, summoned Ahmed and instructed him to take it down to the jailer.

Then Angel phoned Watts & Wainwright, the estate agents, and was soon speaking to Wilf Wainwright again.

'Have you had an approach about 6 Orchard Grove from a man called Nigel Oates in Warrington?' Angel said.

'Yes, Inspector, as a matter of fact he was one of the first inquiries we had way back in December last year.'

'Yet you still haven't sold the property?'

'No. It's a matter of price, Inspector. He has made a rather low offer which was not acceptable to the vendors.'

'Right, Mr Wainwright, what's the situation with Oates now?'

'There are a couple of other prospective purchasers but at the moment, none of them seem eager to pay the asking price. But it's a highly desirable property, I'm in little doubt that we will sell it at the asking price or very near, when we get vacant possession on 1 June.'

'Thank you very much, Mr Wainwright.'

Angel ended the call and replaced the phone.

He rubbed the lobe of his ear between finger and thumb as he thought about Emily Cole. The call to the estate agents about her brother seemed to clear her from any suspicion, which left Angel without a suspect again. He gritted his teeth. He was furious that the murderer had led him by the nose to suspect Cliff Grant, when the man was clearly innocent. Angel felt that the case was slipping away from him. He had to keep a grip on all the evidence gathered so far. If any of it was doubtful, it should be checked and rechecked. Thank goodness he still had one line of inquiry. He was still expecting that somebody on the force was going to spot the red Polo soon. And it was beginning to look as if he would be owing Daniel Ashton the full price of £800, which he hadn't got for the ring for Mary. There were only two days left. Their anniversary was on Thursday.

He heard the church clock chime. He looked at his watch. It was five o'clock. He'd had enough of Tuesday. It had been a wasted day. He'd released one suspect and absolved another. And now he hadn't a suspect in mind. Worse than that. He knew that he could expect another woman aged around sixty years to be murdered between five and eight tomorrow morning, but if not, then the morning after. It was one of those times when he was out of love with Michael Angel. With an expression of a sick toad, he reached out for his hat and went home.

SEVENTEEN

It was 7 p.m. that same Tuesday evening, 12 May 2015.

The delightful Mary had served up an agreeable tea, then after coffee, when they were settled in their chairs, she switched on the TV and played back an old recording of *Bad Girls* which Angel seemed to be enjoying. However, by the time the second commercial break interrupted the programme, she noticed he was fast asleep. She also noted that on the table between them, his mobile phone was open and switched on.

She didn't disturb him. She let the recording continue and went into the kitchen to clear away, wash up and set breakfast.

At ten o'clock she returned, stopped the playback and tuned into the news. The loud introductory music woke Angel, who promptly reached out for his mobile. He blinked at the LCD, put it back on the table, looked at Mary and said, 'Oh. Hello.'

She raised her eyebrows, glanced at the clock on the mantelshelf and said, 'You fell asleep.'

'Oh?' he said with a yawn. 'Sorry, love.' He noticed the clock, then looked at his watch. 'Ten o'clock. Is that the time?' He gestured towards the TV screen and added, 'What happened to her then? Miriam or Marlene or whatever her name was?'

'Maureen. That tall, bullying girl arranged to meet her down the cellar where she battered her to death with an iron bar, then the bully and her skinny friend tried to make it look like she'd escaped.'

'Oh,' he said. He picked up his mobile and seemed uncertain what to do with it.

Mary saw him and said, 'Are you expecting a call?'

He hesitated before replying. 'More like *hoping* for a call, love,' he said.

Her eyes flashed. 'What? At *this* time?' she said.

'I've got the force looking for a particular car.'

Her face tightened. Her eyes narrowed. 'So you'll be getting up again in the middle of the night to make an arrest, I expect?'

He shrugged.

'It's to do with that murderer of those four women, isn't it?' she said.

'The car's probably locked away in some garage for the night. But either way, it's nothing to worry about. There'll be scores of other men with me.'

'Yes, but you're the boss. They expect you to lead them. And you're so *stupidly* brave.'

Her eyes caught the light and Angel saw that they were moist. He hadn't wanted to upset her — he loved her so much. He reached out and put his arms round her.

'There, there,' he said, as one might say to a child.

She struggled angrily to be free of the embrace and said, 'And besides that, I know what a great big show off you are!'

It was 3.45 a.m., Wednesday morning, 13 May. Lucky for some.

The sky was as black as an undertaker's cravat. There was no hooting of owls. No barking of dogs. It was as quiet as death.

The only sounds to be heard in the front bedroom of the Angel homestead were the ticking of the clock and the steady, regular breathing of two people asleep.

Suddenly Angel's mobile phone rang. His eyes shot open. His heart began to thump. In the dark, he rolled over and reached out to the bedside table, found the phone, switched it on and put it to his ear.

A man's voice said, 'DI Angel?'

Angel cupped his hand over the phone, hoping not to wake Mary. 'Yes. Who is this?'

'Patrolman PC Donohue, sir. I've found that little red Polo car you're looking for, sir.'

Angel's heart beat faster. 'Hold on,' he whispered.

He whipped back the duvet, swivelled round, pushed his feet into his slippers, stood up and made his way through the darkness of the bedroom, grabbing his dressing gown off a chair on the way. He crossed the landing to the bathroom, put on the light and closed the door.

'You're in a marked car, aren't you?' Angel said. 'I hope the driver hasn't seen you. Have you got the registration number?'

'My car's well out of the way, sir. I've checked out the registration number. It's in the name of a Mrs Robinson, 12 Fountain Street.'

He frowned. He didn't know anybody called Robinson and he couldn't remember where Fountain Street was.

Angel said, 'It's Sean Donohue, isn't it?'

'Yes, sir,' the PC said, pleased that Angel remembered his Christian name.

'Sean, we *are* talking about an almost new red Polo with a dent and a few scratches in the centre under the number plate at the rear, aren't we?' he said.

'Oh yes, sir. This car ticks all the boxes.'

'Great stuff,' he said. 'Right, is Fountain Street that cul-de-sac off Canal Street?'

'Yes, sir.'

'And where are you?'

'I'm on foot on the corner of Fountain Street and Canal Street.'

'Stay there, Sean. But keep out of sight. I'll be with you in about ten minutes.'

Angel ended the call then scrolled down to DS Crisp and clicked on it. The call went straight to his mailbox. Angel's face muscles tightened. His eyes looked despairingly at the ceiling.

He ground his teeth briefly as he promptly scrolled to DS Carter. It rang for a long time before she answered.

'Hello, yes?' she said with a yawn.

'DI Angel here, Flora. Sorry to wake you. Emergency. That red Polo has been found outside 12 Fountain Street off Canal Street. Can you meet me there ASAP?'

'Yes, sir,' she said. 'It'll take me a few minutes.'

Angel closed the phone, dressed quickly and went downstairs.

Minutes later he was on Wakefield Road. He pulled up short of the turn onto Canal Street and finished the last 200 yards on foot.

As he reached the turning to Fountain Street, a figure in black emerged from a house doorway.

Angel turned back to face him.

'It's me, sir.' It was Patrolman Donohue.

'Ah,' Angel said. 'Where's the red Polo, Sean?'

Donohue peered round the corner. A lone lamp post gave enough illumination to show the reflection of the roofs of about a dozen cars parked on the street.

'It's the second car up on the right,' he said. 'Outside number 12. That's Mrs Robinson's address.'

'I'm going in there,' Angel said.

Donohue's eyebrows shot up. He knew Angel wouldn't have had time to get a warrant. 'It's risky, sir.'

'You don't have to come, Sean. But I have to make the arrest. I'm not taking the risk of any more murders. You push off then and continue with your usual duties.'

'I can't leave you, sir. How do you propose to gain access?'

'I don't know until I see how the windows and door are secured. I've brought a glass cutter, a set of lock picks and . . . look, Sean, I'm wasting time. You get off and continue with your usual duties.'

'No. I'm coming with you, sir.'

'Only if you are sure.'

Donohue stepped round the corner onto Fountain Street. 'Come on, sir.'

Angel smiled and followed him.

They arrived outside number 12. Angel shone his torch at the window catch. He thought it looked easy.

'Give me a bunk up,' he whispered.

Angel was soon on the window sill. He took the glass cutter out of his pocket and cut a small arc in the pane of glass round the window lock. Then he tapped the glass within the arc out with the handle of the cutter. The glass mostly went inwards. Some clattered noisily down into a sink. The racket caused the muscles on the faces of the two men to tighten. However, time was the enemy, so undiminished, Angel put his fingers through the hole in the pane and moved the catch through ninety degrees. He climbed down onto the pavement and between them, Angel and Donohue managed to push the bottom window upward. Angel climbed in.

He scrambled over the sink and found himself not surprisingly in the kitchen. Donohue followed. They shone their torches round the little room. There was the conventional kitchen furniture. They found a door leading to the stairs and the front room, which contained no sign of life.

Angel indicated that he intended investigating upstairs. Donohue kept close behind him. They noiselessly made their way up the stairs to the landing and found the bathroom on their left. To the right were two doors both closed. Angel put his hand on the handle of the first door, pressed it and went in. They flashed their lights around the room. There was a double bed with the bedclothes crumpled and untidy. He put his hand down the bed to check the temperature. It was stone cold. Donohue looked under the bed. Angel opened the wardrobe. He saw clothes for both sexes on hangers in there. He closed the wardrobe doors. They had looked in every place where anybody might have hidden.

Both men went back onto the landing. There was only one more room. Angel opened the door and they went in. It was a very tiny room. Again, they shone their lights around the room. There was nobody there. It was mostly crammed with boxes and suitcases. He noticed incongruously placed on a pile of tea chests was a small wooden crate with a single cauliflower in it. The fact that there was only one made him think. He would have expected two cauliflowers to be in there. It worried him. Next to it was a small, white linen sack he put a hand in and pulled out a handful of dried rice. He shouldn't have been surprised, but he was. There was a small table piled with various papers facing the window, and a chair behind it.

Angel turned to Donohue and said, 'There's nobody here, Sean. We don't have to whisper anymore. Might as well put the light on. See if it works.'

Donohue pressed the switch and the light filled the room. Angel looked round, uncomfortable in these surroundings. Then he suddenly realized something.

'Of *course,* Mrs Robinson isn't here,' he said.

Donohue stared at him.

'There's only one cauliflower here, because she's out killing some other poor woman, the *fifth* on her murder list.' Mac had said that they were murdered between five and eight a.m. He looked at his watch. It was almost 4.30.

Angel crossed to the desk and looked at the papers. On the top of the pile was a photograph. His heart began to race. 'Look at this,' he said.

It was apparently a publicity photograph for "Grounds for Divorce". There were about sixteen pretty girls scantily dressed. Somebody had ringed six of them round their heads. Four of those had red crosses across their faces. The names of the girls were given underneath. He recognized the women who had red crosses over their faces. He read out their names, as they were listed on the photograph.

'Look, Sean,' he said. 'There's Gladys Hemingway, Fay Mitchell, Felicity Oakenshaw and Michele Noble. They're all dead. The other two are ringed, but not yet crossed out in red . . . therefore *one* of them must be her next target.'

Donohue was looking over Angel's shoulder.

'What are their names, sir?' he said.

'Melanie Mackinley and Lorna Bainbridge. But if they married their surnames would have changed.'

Angel turned the photograph over. 'Bingo!' he said. 'It's all here. All laid out for us. There's the full list of the six, with their maiden names, their married names and their addresses.'

'You've hit the jackpot, sir.'

'Write this down, Sean, quickly. Melanie Mackinley, now Melanie Hooper of 26 Upper Sheffield Road, Bromersley and Lorna Bainbridge, now Lorna Powell of 17 Wath Road, Bromersley.'

Angel then checked his watch. It was 4.35 a.m. He waited patiently while Donohue hurriedly entered the names and addresses in his notebook.

Then suddenly both of them heard a slight noise of someone moving around downstairs.

They looked at each other. Angel's heart began to pound. He pointed to a place of concealment behind a stack of boxes. Donohue nodded and took up the position. Angel switched out the light and dodged behind the door which had been wide open. He pushed it to the almost closed position and waited.

Seconds later the landing light went on and they heard footsteps on the stairs. Then the door was pushed open, and the room light went on. Angel peered through the gap in the door hinge and immediately recognized the prowler. It was DS Carter.

Angel sighed with relief.

'Come in, Flora,' he said, stepping out from behind the door. 'I'd almost forgotten about you.'

Her eyebrows shot up, she gasped and put a hand on her chest. 'Oh, sir!'

Donohue came out from behind the boxes. They looked at each other and nodded.

Angel said, 'Listen up, Flora, and you, Sean, time is very short. I believe that the murderer will be at one of these two addresses, but there's no way of knowing which.' He looked down at the back of the photograph he was holding and said, 'If you two will check on Melanie Mackinley — oh, it's Hooper now — on Upper Sheffield Road. Check that she is safe, and stay with her until after 8 a.m. I'll take on the other one, Lorna Powell on Wath Road. Neither address is far away. Let's hope we're not too late. All right?'

Both Carter and Donohue's eyes shone in anticipation of what they had to do. Angel saw this and said, 'Be very careful. You might meet the very devil incarnate. Somebody who you may already know, who has killed four innocent women in cold blood and who will have no conscience in murdering either or both of you.'

Carter looked at Angel. His eyes were hard. His chin set firm. She realized he was absolutely in earnest.

'We'll be careful, sir,' she said.

'One more thing,' he appealed to her, 'I haven't any handcuffs. Do you think—'

Flora said, 'Take mine, sir,' she said, dipping into the back pocket of her jeans. 'Sean has a pair on his belt.'

Donohue nodded. 'Yep. That's fine, Sarge.'

Angel pocketed the handcuffs and said, 'Come on. Let's go!'

Angel turned out the room light, then they all scrambled downstairs, out of the house and raced to their respective cars.

Angel made his way to 17 Wath Road, which was only two or three minutes away.

Because the roads were empty, the traffic lights conveniently changed to green as the BMW approached so that he soon arrived at his destination.

Like Fountain Street, Wath Road was made up of one short block of terraced houses. He parked the car at the end of the street and ran up to number 17. He had to obtain access, silently but quickly. He shone the torch on the rear downstairs window, and saw that it had not been tampered with, then he looked at the door. His heart missed a beat. On the door jamb, just above and below the keyhole were damage marks and splintered wood where a crowbar or similar had been used to prise the door open. They were similar to the marks found on the doors of the victims. It was further confirmation that the murderer was in or had recently been in the house.

Angel's pulse shot up. His chest was on fire. He tried the door. It opened easily. He went inside and silently closed it. He thought he could hear someone talking. It was a muttered monotone coming from upstairs. He quickly made his way through the kitchen to the stairs. He slowly and quietly began to climb them.

He could hear a man's voice. It was saying, '. . . and you were one of the reasons. All my life I've had to put up with rejection after rejection by you and others like you. You are the fifth, next to the last of the women I have been able to trace from that disgusting, group sexual display you called dancing. You don't know how much you fired my desire. I was positively burning up with a craving for you, but when I suggested that I took *you* out on a date, you laughed at me and looked down on me, as if I was scum. I knew you had been talking to the others about me. I thought I would be able to date you, take you to a smart hotel, wine and dine you then take you to a bed and love you and caress you. We could have had a wonderful sexual relationship. I had, still have, a fantastic body, in terrific shape, and a six pack to be proud of but you just laughed at me, like the others. You'd rather throw yourselves at those overfed, bald, spotty, obnoxious creeps. There I was, helpless, lonely, miserable, suffering rejection and enduring all my unfulfilled desires. And it went on and on.

'As I got older, I realized how much I had missed . . . not being able to get a girlfriend, never mind a wife. You and your friends made a fool of me. You laughed at me. Now it's my turn. If you had married me, I would have worshipped you, covered you in flowers. There's one. It's a cauliflower. Laugh at that! Hold it on your lap, like a bouquet, Lorna. That's it.

Now, laugh at that! And later, when you come out of church, there will be plenty of confetti and rice. Particularly rice. In fact, you'll get fed up with rice. You'll feel all choked up. Yes. There's another laugh. All choked up. Laugh at that, Lorna!'

Angel was now on the landing. He could see the light from the open bedroom door. The voice was loud and clear.

'I've even written a poem about you, Lorna, so that the cops will know it's me. Would you like to hear it?' He waited a second then said, 'I'll take that as a yes. It goes like this:

Lorna Powell ridiculed me many and many and many a time.
And has to be punished for her wicked crime.'

A grin spread across his face.

'Clever, isn't it?' he continued. 'And you're the fifth, Lorna. Just one more to go.'

Then Angel heard a woman's voice, obviously that of Lorna Powell, trembling as she said, 'You're mad. Raving mad. As mad as a hatter. You need a doctor.'

Angel heard the man suck in breath between his teeth, enraged by what she had said.

'I don't need a frigging doctor,' the man said. 'I just need a fair deal out of this life that you and all your sex have denied me. How could those ugly lumps of so-called men so easily get themselves a woman when I couldn't? Women must be stupid. I am attractive, well-educated with a fantastic body. They have starved me of sex during my young and middle-aged manhood and given that pleasure to other men. Why do I have to suffer virginity all my life? Why is this? I am almost a living god, yet nobody realizes it. I will cleanse the world eventually of all that is perverted and imperfect. It will happen. I have decreed it. Until then, I have to face a miserable, lonely, celibate life where everyone else experiences the pleasures of sex and love. It is the darkest hell that you have *never* experienced — but now it is *your* turn.'

Lorna Powell screamed. '*No*! *No*!'

The shrill note stirred Angel to action, although he had no idea what he was going to do. He dashed into the bedroom.

He saw what he thought was the back view of a woman with grey hair in a sheepskin coat, sitting on a bed, facing a woman he took to be Lorna Powell in a nightdress in bed. The one with grey hair was holding a knife with a shiny blade at least ten inches long, about to plunge it into Mrs Powell.

'Put that knife down,' Angel said. 'I am a policeman.'

The killer jumped up, turned round and Angel saw a tall, heavily made-up man with excesses of blue and black grease-paint around his eyes and carmine on his lips, and a grey wig that had gone askew. Angel blinked with shock at the grotesque sight. He was certain that he knew the face behind the make-up, but he couldn't put him into context. Then it came to him. It was the bread man who delivered to Grant's shop!

'You're Maddison,' Angel said. 'So-called friend of Cliff Grant.'

Angel was furious with himself. It had chiefly been Maddison's evidence that he had seen a woman with grey hair entering Grant's shop that had persuaded him that the handwriting expert must be wrong and that the murderer was a woman!

Maddison's face was perspiring through the make-up. The corners of his mouth were turned downwards. He bared his teeth like a wild dog. 'I have no friends, Mr Policeman. Grant was just a pawn in the game.'

'A pawn, friend, call him what you like,' Angel said. 'You created fake evidence to fool me into thinking *he* was the killer.'

Maddison laughed long and loud. 'Yes, and you fell for it.'

Angel wasn't amused. 'You even sold him the ring you had stolen from Michelle Pulman and swore him to secrecy,' he said. 'He never betrayed that promise, you know.'

Maddison laughed again. 'He was so gullible.'

'What had you against him?'

'Everything. I saw him and I hated everything about him. He had the power over women that was due to me as their god. He had only to crook a finger at a woman and she came running towards him. He always seemed to have at least two women chasing him at any given time. But they were chasing the wrong man. They should have been looking at me, and one day soon, they will. But now, Angel, I have to eliminate you.'

Maddison suddenly lunged at him with the knife, and Angel had to back off. The man stabbed the air again and again but Angel managed to dodge his jabs. At the same time, Angel reached out and attempted to grab the wrist that held the knife. Maddison chased him round the bedroom, attempting to stab him at every opportunity. Eventually Angel managed to catch that wrist with both hands. But with his free hand, Maddison landed some exceedingly heavy blows with his clenched fist at Angel's temple and on his neck. Angel now had his back against the bedroom wall. Blow after blow rained down on him, until he managed to dodge Maddison's mightiest blow and his bare knuckles hit the bedroom wall, making a solid noise and causing him to cry out.

Angel wasn't sure whether Maddison had broken his wrist, damaged a finger or merely battered his knuckles. In the split second that the killer was coming to terms with the pain, Angel banged the other hand holding the knife on the corner of the wardrobe. Maddison yelled again as the knife fell onto the carpet. He quickly went down for it, Angel powerfully brought up his knee, caught him under the chin, and his teeth met as he sent him flying backwards. The grey wig slid off his head. Maddison staggered backwards towards the wall and as he fell, he hit the back of his head on a radiator which stunned him. He was dazed long enough for Angel to roll him onto his stomach, pull his arms behind his back and snap the handcuffs on his wrists.

He then turned to Mrs Powell. She was sat up in bed with a floral duvet wrapped tightly round her. She was shaking slightly. Her face was white. He could see that she must have been very beautiful forty years ago.

Angel looked at her and said, 'Are you all right?'

She smiled weakly. 'I'm fine. You must be that Inspector Angel, the one that always gets his man, like the Mounties.'

He looked away from her and said, 'Something like that.'

He sat on the edge of the bed, swept the hair off his face and took out his mobile. Although his neck and shoulder were considerably painful, he wasn't about to let Mrs Powell realize the punishment he had taken. He managed to keep his hand from rubbing the area and concentrated on finding the number of the Control Room. He found it and clicked on the button.

'Control Room, DS Clifton.'

He was relieved when he heard a voice he recognized.

'DI Angel, Bernie. Will you send a car and two men to 17 Wath Road, to collect a prisoner? His name is Percy Maddison. He needs to be charged with the murder of four women, which will then need to be processed.'

Clifton was delighted. 'Great stuff, sir,' he said. 'I'll see to that personally.'

Angel could hear the pleasure in his voice.

'Congratulations,' Clifton said then added in a concerned voice, 'Are you all right, sir?'

'Of course,' Angel said quickly.

'Two men and a car will be there within five minutes, sir.'

Angel checked his watch. It was seven o'clock. 'Thanks, Bernie. I will wait to hand him over to your men but I won't be accompanying the prisoner. You don't need me. Ahmed has all the details of the victims and so on.'

'Right, sir,' Clifton said.

Then Angel remembered that Ahmed had an appointment with the Chief Constable that morning, and he was worried about it. So he told Clifton, 'Incidentally, will you tell Ahmed I will be going home . . . to catch up with some sleep for one thing. I shall be going to the bank, Daniel Ashton's antique shop, then the card shop next door. But I'll be in later this morning.'

EIGHTEEN

Angel was elated as he drove the car into his garage and then strode out, seemingly weightlessly, down the garden path. He was smiling as he let himself into the house by the back door. Then he began softly to hum, 'I did it my way,' as he took off his coat, hung it up in the hall cupboard. He observed that there was no sign anywhere of Mary downstairs. He listened and there was no sound of movement or running water upstairs either. It would suit his plans very well, if she stayed in bed another hour or so.

He switched the radio on low volume so it wouldn't wake her, then quickly made some tea in a beaker, loaded a slice of bread in the toaster, and took out the butter dish and the marmalade jar from the cupboard. When he had finished his breakfast, he prepared fresh tea and hot toast and took it up to Mary on a tray. She was delighted but didn't say anything about their wedding anniversary, so neither did he. He came down the stairs wondering if she had forgotten but then thought that was highly unlikely knowing her as he did. Anyway, he had told her he was going to the station as usual, but first he went down town to the bank, Ashton's antique shop, the card shop, the florists for some flowers and then went to the police station.

Everybody smiled at Angel as he went down the corridor. The news about the arrest of Percy Maddison for the serial killer murders had spread very quickly.

Angel arrived in his office and checked the time. It was 10.20. It was about the time that he expected Ahmed to be coming out of the Chief Constable's office. He smiled as he thought about it.

The phone went. He reached out for it. It was Mary.

'Yes, sweetheart,' he said. 'What's the matter?'

She said, 'Michael, do you realize that this is our wedding anniversary?'

'Yes,' he said. 'Of course I do. I thought you had forgotten.'

'Well,' she said, 'you didn't mention it and you didn't even kiss me. I should have thought as it is twenty-four years since we walked down the aisle together that you wouldn't have forgotten.'

'Of course I haven't forgotten. And it's twenty-*five* years, sweetheart, not twenty-four. It's our *silver* wedding anniversary.'

'No, Michael. That's *next* year. It might seem to be twenty-five to you, darling, but it's only actually twenty-four . . . You work it out.'

Angel did the sum quickly in his head and discovered that she was right.

'Erm . . . well, however many years it is,' he said, 'I still hadn't forgotten. And I still love you. And I'll be home early, all being well.'

Her tone and attitude changed. 'Oh,' she said. 'And I still love you, Michael. Look forward to it.'

They ended the call. He replaced the phone.

Angel was pleased she had phoned. But he needn't have worried about that solitaire ring if he had realized he had had another year to save up for it.

There was a knock at the door.

Angel thought he knew who it would be and smiled in anticipation. He called out, 'Come in.'

It *was* Ahmed.

He had a huge smile on his face. He had had his hair cut and was wearing his best suit; a crisp white shirt, blue tie and black shoes so highly polished that you could see your face in them. He strutted into the office and closed the door.

Angel looked at him. 'What's the Cheshire Cat smile for, Ahmed? Is it because we now have to call you Detective *Sergeant* Ahaz?'

THE END

ALSO BY ROGER SILVERWOOD

YORKSHIRE MURDER MYSTERIES

Book 1: THE MISSING NURSE
Book 2: THE MISSING WIFE
Book 3: THE MAN IN THE PINK SUIT
Book 4: THE MORALS OF A MURDERER
Book 5: THE AUCTION MURDERS
Book 6: THE MISSING KILLER
Book 7: THE UMBRELLA MURDERS
Book 8: THE MISSING MILLIONAIRE
Book 9: THE MISSING THIEF
Book 10: FIND THE LADY
Book 11: THE MISSING MODEL
Book 12: MURDER IN BARE FEET
Book 13: THE MISSING HUSBAND
Book 14: THE CUCKOO CLOCK MURDERS
Book 15: SHRINE TO MURDER
Book 16: THE SNUFFBOX MURDERS
Book 17: THE DOG COLLAR MURDERS
Book 18: THE CHESHIRE CAT MURDERS
Book 19: THE DIAMOND ROSARY MURDERS
Book 20: THIRTEEN STEPS TO MURDER
Book 21: THE FRUIT GUM MURDERS
Book 22: THE MONEY TREE MURDERS
Book 23: ANGEL AND THE ACTRESS
Book 24: THE MURDER LIST

Thank you for reading this book.

If you enjoyed it please leave feedback on Amazon or Goodreads, and if there is anything we missed or you have a question about, then please get in touch. The author and publishing team appreciate your feedback and time reading this book.

We're very grateful to eagle-eyed readers who take the time to contact us. Please send any errors you find to corrections@joffebooks.com. We'll get them fixed ASAP.

Printed in Great Britain
by Amazon

46291853R00118